OPERATION
YES

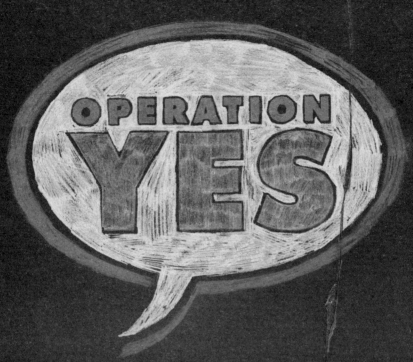

SARA LEWIS HOLMES

SCHOLASTIC INC.

NEW YORK   TORONTO   LONDON   AUCKLAND
SYDNEY   MEXICO CITY   NEW DELHI   HONG KONG

No part of this publication may be reproduced, stored in a retrieval system, or transmitted in any form or by any means, electronic, mechanical, photocopying, recording, or otherwise, without written permission of the publisher. For information regarding permission, write to Scholastic Inc., Attention: Permissions Department, 557 Broadway, New York, NY 10012.

ISBN 978-0-545-10796-9

Arthur A. Levine Books hardcover edition designed by Phil Falco, published by Arthur A. Levine Books, an imprint of Scholastic Inc., September 2009.

12 11 10 9 8 7 6 5 4   18 19/0

Printed in the U.S.A.   40
This edition first printing, July 2012

Lyrics from "Anthem" by Leonard Cohen © 1992 by Leonard Cohen. Used by permission.

The display type was set in Futura.
The text type was set in Futura.

For Rebecca and Wade,
who are both
Courage and Kindness

CONTENTS

PLAN

A

TO THOSE WHO JUST ARRIVED:

Listen up, New Recruit. This is a Work In Progress.
Like me. Like you. We are all capital W... capital I... capital P.

But before we head out, you need to know where you are,
who's with you in this battle,
and why you should say yes.

The same things we all want to know on Day One.

1
DAY ONE

On the first day of school, Miss Loupe approached the left edge of the front row of her first-ever sixth-grade classroom. Before her new students' eyes, she knelt and stuck one end of a giant roll of beige tape to the floor at their feet. Then she crept backward on her knees, tacking the three-inch-wide strip of tape to the heavily waxed linoleum. As she moved away from them, toward the cracked chalkboard that hung on the front wall, the tape unspooled in a straight line.

The students gawked. Their teacher was a trim woman with confident shoulders, a clean face, and an amazing total of twelve tiny hoops hugging the curves of her ears, but she still looked ridiculous, because her head was below their feet and her khaki-clad rear was bobbing up and down. They would have started whispering and poking and giggling, except that Miss Loupe began calling the roll.

Bo Whaley (*Here. What's up with the tape?*)
Melissa Paperwhite (*Yes, ma'am, I'm here, ma'am.*)
Martina Abucay (*Here.*)

She wasn't going in alphabetical order, she wasn't using a computer-generated class roster, and she wasn't stumbling over any of the pronunciations. The names simply floated up from the floor randomly, like she was drawing raffle prizes.

Rick Konchak   (*Here. Do I have to sit up front?*)
Trey Obermeyer   (*Reporting for duty, ma'am.*)

Bo gave Trey a virtual high five in the space between their desks. He thought Miss Loupe would look up at Trey's response, but she didn't. How was she going to know which face went with which name?

When she reached the front wall, Miss Loupe tore off the end of the tape and patted it firmly to the floor. Then she attached a new piece of tape on top of that spot and resumed crawling, this time parallel to the chalkboard. Bo, Trey, and the rest of the back row had to lean out of their seats to see what she was doing. One corner of her teal-blue shirt came untucked and trailed along beside her. The class could see a tattoo of a bird on her left hip.

Sanjay Pavore   (*Yes.*)
Kylie Davidson   (*Here.*)
Lisa DeFazio   (*Silence.*)
(*Not here, ma'am. She moved to Texas, ma'am, to Randolph Air Force Base. Her father got promoted.*)

When she reached the far right corner of the room, where her desk was, Miss Loupe (and her roll of tape) switched directions again and inched slowly backward toward her students. They could see the white zigzags on the soles of her shoes. She called ten more names, including:

Aimee Ortiz   (*I'm here. Do you need help with that?*)
Zachary Nolan   (*Zac.*)
Shaunelle Camden   (*Here. Um, I'm new . . .*)

Below their desks, Miss Loupe and her roll of tape changed course a final time. She crept past the toes of the entire front row, unreeling and anchoring a straight line of tape to the floor just beyond their feet. Everyone in the front row saw the mole behind her right ear, and Martina noticed how her hair changed from deep brown to white blond as it rose from the nape of her neck to the spiky crown of her head. The boys in the back couldn't see anything, but they hoped Rick at the front would report any more tattoos.

Dillon Sanchez   (*Did they tell you I'm moving? I'm moving.*)
Allison Yancey   (*I'm here above you, Miss Loupe. You know, in the center?*)

Finally, Miss Loupe reached the spot where she had started her journey and the end of her string of names. Patting the last strip of tape firmly onto the corner of the rectangle that now occupied the entire front of her classroom, she rose to her feet, placed the giant roll of tape around her slim wrist, and addressed the class.

"WHERE AM I?" she asked, throwing her arms out wide.

The gesture made her appear a bit taller, but still, she was no bigger than a fourth grader. A fourth grader with a belly ring, which was twinkling in plain view now that her arms had freed the last edges of her shirt from her belt.

The class sat in stunned silence.

She repeated her words, her voice filling the room as if she were the announcer at the annual air show. "WHERE AM I?"

The students rustled with unease. Wasn't their teacher supposed to say: "Welcome to the sixth grade, and I'm very, very glad you're here, but as the top grade at Young Oaks, you have a responsibility to the rest of the school to set a good example"? Were they supposed to completely ignore her belly ring? Could they ask about her tattoo? And why would a teacher put tape on the floor?

Bo wanted to ask all of these questions and more. But Miss Loupe had asked her question first, and now she belted it out one more time: "WHERE AM I?"

What kind of a question was that? In the last six years, Bo had moved five times. He'd never had a teacher who was newer to a school than he was, and they'd all known exactly where they were. But if there was one thing he'd learned in all the moves he'd made, it was to not mess up and ask the wrong questions on the first day of school. Teachers had long memories, and they told other teachers about you too.

Finally, Bo decided that a brand-new teacher with a belly ring would not have a rule about raising your hand before speaking (he turned out to be wrong about that), and he called out: "Aren't you in Room 208?"

"Yes. Yes, of course, I am. But *where* in Room 208 am I?" Miss Loupe used her upturned palms to mimic the outline of tape.

"You're in a rectangle, ma'am?" ventured Melissa. She had opened her binder, her pencil poised.

"Let me give you a hint," Miss Loupe said. She walked to the middle of the marked-off space. She placed the roll of tape flat on the floor. Then she began to circle it, eyeing it from all angles. She squatted with one hand held above her eyes, as if she were shielding them from bright sun. Then she stood to one side of the tape, about six feet away, and grasped an imaginary stick, gently drew it backward —

"YOU'RE PUTTING!!!" Bo burst out. "It's a golf course and you're on the green, you're going for a birdie. . . ." Melissa turned to look at him, and he yanked his hand back down. "You're putting," he muttered.

Miss Loupe's head popped up from her downward gaze at the imaginary golf club. "Yes! Thanks for the vote of confidence in my game. I usually don't score birdies . . . more like triple bogies. Do you play golf?"

Bo shrugged. He and Trey liked to mess around with the old clubs they had bought at the base thrift shop, mostly in the rough field behind Trey's house where the mobile home park used to be. There were concrete slabs and rusty metal drains that made balls shoot up into the air like popcorn. But he just said, "Putting

5

greens aren't square. They're mostly round. Your tape looks more like a tee box to me."

"Yes, you're right. Maybe I'm not on the golf course after all." Melissa crossed out the words *Golf. Putting. Birdie.* on her paper.

Miss Loupe threw up her hands. "So WHERE am I?"

This time, she walked to the back of the Taped Space, sat down, and huddled against the wall below the chalkboard. At his seat, Bo rose up onto his knees so he could see her. Miss Loupe's shoulders sagged, her head dropped to her bent legs, and her hands hung limply near her curled feet. The room seemed to darken, as if the formerly bright sun had weakened to a dim glow. The class could hear the ragged edges of her breath. They shifted in their seats, unsure.

Miss Loupe's head tilted up. She crawled to the middle of the floor where she had left the roll of tape and cupped her hands around it like a bowl. She lifted it weakly to her lips.

"You're a dog in the pound!" Zac said. The girls all glared at him.

Miss Loupe didn't answer.

"Prison!" said Melissa, waving her pencil. "You're a POV!"

"I think you mean, like, POW," said Allison, who was sitting in front of Melissa. She flipped her long brown hair out of her eyes. "Like my grandfather. He was a prisoner of war in Vietnam. He was interviewed on TV about it and they, like, even made this movie about him —"

"Yes, thank you, Allison," Miss Loupe said from the floor. "You are correct. POVs are privately owned vehicles, while POWs are, as you said, brave people."

Allison smoothed the ends of her hair so they curled against her silky pink sweater. Bo wondered if her grandfather had really been a POW. Last year, when he'd first gotten to this school, he had believed Allison when she told the whole fifth grade that her older brother was with the CIA in Afghanistan. Thanks to Trey, who had been at Young Oaks since kindergarten, Bo now knew she didn't have an older brother, only a little one named Tony in first grade, who told everyone *his* big sister was an exchange student in Rome.

Miss Loupe stood up again and threw her arms out wide.

"WHERE AM I?" she said.

This time, Bo didn't wait for her to start pantomiming.

"You're on stage!" he called out.

Miss Loupe grinned and nodded her head, which made her earrings flash.

"Welcome to the Taped Space!"

She reached down, picked up the roll of tape, and tossed it over three rows of desks to where Bo was sitting. It bounced off the wall behind him and dropped into his hands.

"The Taped Space is also known as the Theatrical Space," Miss Loupe continued, "or our Temporary Stage."

She turned around and wrote in block letters on the chalkboard:

ART NEEDS A FRAME

And below that:

ART IS ARRANGING OBJECTS TO CREATE BEAUTY

She turned back to her students.

"This isn't art class. This is sixth grade. I know that. But when I was in sixth grade, I lived here in Reform, because my dad was an instructor pilot on the base. I went to class in this exact same school, and . . ." She paused. "Principal Heard was my sixth-grade teacher."

"Really?" said Bo. "Was she big then too?"

The class busted out laughing, but Bo's own grin faded quickly. His teacher was tight with the principal? He hadn't planned on seeing Mrs. Heard so often this year — in fact, not at all. His dad had been clear about that.

Miss Loupe held up her hand.

"Not as . . . substantial," she admitted. "But she was a great teacher. And she could draw anything. You know that map of the U.S. in the main hallway? Mrs. Heard painted that."

When? thought Bo. *In the Stone Age?* The colors on the map had faded so much that the cows in Wisconsin looked more gray than brown, and part of the coast of California had worn away.

"I'm not good at drawing like she is," Miss Loupe continued. "She wanted to hire a teacher who could create murals like that map and spruce things up around here. But I talked her into taking a chance on me."

She looked around her class, at each face, as if she were marveling that she was there in Room 208 with them.

"Because I do know something about another kind of art," she said. "Theater."

She turned back to the board and wrote one more thing:

THEATER IS THE ART OF SAYING YES

"But ma'am," said Melissa, waving her hand like a crossing guard, "how do we do that?"

Miss Loupe lifted a pile of Student Handbooks.

"Tomorrow," she said. "Today, the Handbook awaits." She gave the books to Rick to pass back.

The class slumped in their chairs. Bo turned the roll of tape around and around in his hands. This was the weirdest Day One he'd ever had.

Miss Loupe smiled confidently at the class. "We have a frame," she said, indicating the boundaries of the Taped Space. "We *are* going to learn regular sixth-grade material. We have to cover the Handbook. But for the rest of the year, we'll also see what happens when we say *yes*."

2
THAT NIGHT, ACROSS THE COUNTRY, IN SEATTLE

No. No. No.

Gari watched her mom make the call. Maybe Bo would pick up and then forget to give the message to his mom and dad.

"Hello, Donna? Oh, it's good to hear your voice! I really need to talk to you and Phil."

Gari imagined one word on a giant billboard outside Aunt Donna's window in North Carolina. (Did they have billboards on Air Force bases? She'd never been on one to know.) But if they did, it should say:

NO

In her head, she wrote the details of her protest across the white space. Say this, Aunt Donna, say this:

No way, no how, not on your life.
Gari CANNOT come stay with us.
It wouldn't work out.
It wouldn't be best.

She thought about adding some loudspeakers to the side of the billboard:

I can't believe you'd let her fly across the country by herself!

What about school? Wasn't Gari accepted to Seattle Junior Academy?

What can you be thinking, heading off to IRAQ with the Army and leaving her with us?

Gari added a scrawl of red paint across the imaginary sign:

No. Please, say no.

3
. . . AND IN NORTH CAROLINA

Bo's mom answered the phone. It was 7:05.

"Yes. Yes. Of course she can," his mom said. "When?"

Then again:

"Yes. Yes. Yes. Don't worry about it, Paula, please. Yes, it'll all be fine. I'll get Phil."

She motioned for Bo to get his dad, who had just come home, and who was sitting, reading glasses on his nose, behind an enormous pile of papers that required his signature as the base commander. When his dad came into the kitchen, Bo's mom covered the receiver with one hand and said, "It's your sister. The Army needs her back. She wants Gari to come live with us." She slipped the phone into his outstretched hand. "I said yes."

Gari? Bo flashed on a memory of a skinny girl who had come on vacation with them at the lake one year. Him, doing a brilliant shark imitation. Her, with a tree branch. Him, on the way to the emergency room, blood pouring down his leg.

"Will they let her on base?" he asked.

"Of course," his mom said. Her eyes followed his dad as he took the phone out onto their deck, where he liked to pace as he talked. "She'll have an ID card. Same as you."

12

"Is she going to be in my class?"

"Probably. We'll work everything out in the next few weeks."

"She won't be here for the air show, will she?"

"Yes, that will be nice. You could show her around."

No way. No way was he sharing that day with her. But instead, he said: "My teacher has a tattoo."

"Hmmm?" his mom replied. She was circling a date on the calendar tacked to their kitchen wall and making a line extending out from it over the numbers that marked the days.

Bo looked out the double doors to the deck. His dad was still pacing and talking.

"How come you didn't ask me?" said Bo.

"Ask you what?" said his mom. She stopped drawing the line and left it, dangling, with a little arrow pointing onward.

"Nothing," said Bo. He opened the fridge and picked up a tub of something brown. Hummus. What was that? Not for his lunch tomorrow, he hoped.

The other phone in the house rang. His dad's official work line. His mom picked it up. She listened and then said to Bo, "Command Post."

He headed out to the deck. His dad was still talking, but he looked quizzically at Bo.

"Command Post," Bo said.

His dad squeezed Bo's shoulder. *Thanks*, he mouthed back.

He knew his dad would call the Command Post as soon he hung up with Aunt Paula. He might have to go out to the flight line. Or make a classified call from Wing Headquarters.

Bo walked back into the kitchen just as the doorbell rang.

"I'll be right there!" his mom called out. "You can walk over to the BX and get pizza," she said to Bo. "Don't forget to feed Indy. I'll be home by nine."

She grabbed a large white binder labeled *Scholarship Planning Committee* and headed for the door.

"I'm sorry," she said to the woman waiting for her. "My sister-in-law called, and . . . oh . . . I'll tell you in the car. Things are always a mile a minute around here. Sometimes, I . . ." She looked back at Bo.

"Thanks," she said.

"For what?"

"Hanging in there," she said. She stepped back a few paces and grabbed her cell phone off the hall table. She whispered to Bo, "It's not a skull and crossbones, is it?"

Bo shook his head. He pointed to his left side. "A bird. Tiny." He was used to his mom finishing conversations with him minutes after he'd started them. She didn't forget or miss much; she just didn't always catch the ball right when he threw it.

Bo didn't walk to the Base Exchange to get pizza. The Command Post call turned out to be the weather station, notifying his dad that there was "lightning within five" — a thunderstorm within five miles of the base. Bo could have told you that from the still, heavy air. And because his dog, Indy, had settled into her spot in front of the double doors to the deck. In August, in North Carolina, a storm rolled through two or three times a week. It was a miracle, his dad said, that the maintainers ever fixed any airplanes on the flight line at night at all.

His dad made scrambled eggs with pickles and toast. They

ate at the kitchen counter and watched a dark tarp of clouds unroll over the sky.

"School good?" asked his dad. "Your teacher okay?"

Bo shrugged. Miss Loupe looked different from any other teacher he'd ever had. She'd put on an entertaining show for a few minutes before going on to be a regular teacher for the rest of the day. But if Mrs. Heard had hired her . . . yeah, AND taught her . . .

"She's okay," he said. "Better than Mr. Nix. But school still stinks."

"As bad as a marine's feet?" his dad teased.

"At least grunts *do* something all day. We just sit there. I hate school." Bo popped a pickle into his mouth and savored its crunchy sourness.

"Hate it or not, I expect better this year."

Bo didn't say anything. Every time he messed up, he not only went to the principal, but his dad also had WORK for him to complete. Scrubbing the driveway. Pruning back the wild, thorny bushes at the edge of their backyard. Cleaning the tops of doors and the back inside corners of kitchen cabinets. "You are a Work In Progress," his parents liked to say. "You work. You make progress."

"No imitating Mrs. Heard," his dad clarified.

He'd only shown those sitting near him how he could mouth along with her words during the morning announcements. If he hadn't stuffed his down jacket under his shirt to look more authentic, Mr. Nix wouldn't have noticed.

"No somersaulting."

He had *wanted* to show Trey how it was possible to jump over a lunch table in a single bound. Wasn't it more responsible to have gently somersaulted over it instead?

"No Private Mishaps, Major Shenanigans . . ." His dad picked up a triangular piece of toast and pretended to make it enter a downward spin in midair.

". . . or General Tomfoolery," Bo finished, grabbing the toast before it crashed into his eggs. "I know."

You try it, he wanted to tell his dad. *Try being as good as everyone thinks the commander's son should be without seeming like you're better than anyone else.* He didn't know if he could be good all the way until next summer, when his dad would get a new assignment from the Air Force. He bent the toast triangle in half, lined it with a triple row of pickles, and stuffed the whole grenade into his mouth. Explosions of sour juice went off as he chewed. School: No loud noises. No cool moves. No making things up. It was all toast and no pickles.

The official phone rang again.

"Besides," said his dad as he got up to answer it, "Gari's going to get here, and she'll be plenty out of sorts. I don't want you setting a poor example."

Bo swallowed his last bite of pickle grenade. He didn't think Gari was going to be fooled if he said he was in love with school. And if that tree branch he remembered was any clue, she could handle herself fine. But his dad was looking at him, waiting for a response before he picked up the phone.

"Yes, sir."

His dad nodded his approval.

"Colonel Whaley," he said crisply into the phone. "Yes, yes. Well, bad news doesn't get better with age. Tell me now."

He started out onto the deck, realized it was pouring, and headed into his home office.

His dad, Bo thought, always said yes. He wished he didn't have to do the same.

4

. . . AND BACK IN SEATTLE

Gari crept out of bed and grabbed her cell phone. She punched 2 for Tandi's home number. It was late, but Tandi would be up. Gari's mom said school had started today in North Carolina, but it hadn't yet in Seattle, at least not for all the good private schools, like Seattle Junior Academy.

"It's for sure now." Gari jumped right in. "The stupid Army needs nurses. They want my mom back. Yeah. A hospital in *Iraq*."

She settled under her covers. It was getting cold again at night. She could hear the rain against her window, pattering quietly. Everything was normal on the outside.

"She said the hospital's on an American base, where she'll be safe. I said, What about the shooting and the rocket attacks and the people who hate us? Is the news just making that up?"

She listened.

"I know. None of it makes sense. And why her?"

She closed her eyes in the dark. Then her eyes were open again. She sat all the way up.

"No, she can't. She CAN'T."

She listened again and then hugged her knees to her chest. Did Tandi want her mom to go to jail?

She said in a fierce whisper, "Well, YOU don't know one thing about the Army, and neither does whoever said that."

She could feel her voice rising but she couldn't stop it.

"When the Army says, *Jump!* you're supposed to say, *How high?* Not: *Wait a sec while I tie my shoe and would you mind if I didn't JUMP AT ALL?*"

Gari flopped back down on her pillow. The back of her neck felt damp, as if she'd left the window open and the rain had come inside. *Why didn't Tandi get it?*

"Sorry. Sorry. Are you still there?"

She changed the subject.

"Look, I can still be your campaign manager. You *will* be class president. I've got these amazing posters planned —"

She forced herself to focus on her great idea for Tandi's posters. She couldn't give a speech for Tandi — the thought of that made her palms sweat. She'd rather eat a bathtub of worms. But she could make the best posters anyone at SeaJA had ever seen.

Vote for Tandi Starr — a light as bright as day!

Wouldn't that look great in phosphorescent paint, glowing on signs all over the school? She'd sketch some plans to show Tandi she was serious.

Her mom might have to jump for the Army, but Gari didn't have to.

"Don't worry. I'll talk to my mom tomorrow. She's got to let me stay."

I'll make it work out. I will.

5
THE QUAGMIRE OF IGNORANCE

It was the next day, the second day of school. The Taped Space (the Theatrical Space, the Temporary Stage) was still there. Waiting.

Bo didn't say a word to the rest of the class about Gari coming. *What's she like?* they would ask. And he would have to say, *Who knows?* People changed from year to year. From month to month. Even from day to day. For example, Miss Loupe. Today, there was no sign of her Day One weirdness. She was acting like she'd never crawled on a floor before and she was doing boring teacher things, like evaluating their math skills.

In the middle of the evaluation, the principal, Mrs. Heard, came into Room 208. She was encased in an olive-green suit, which Trey instantly began to draw, adding tank treads and a firing turret.

"I hate to interrupt your lesson, Carol — ah, Miss Loupe," she said, her body filling the entire frame of the doorway, "but this can't wait."

She handed Miss Loupe a thick packet of papers.

"Colonel Whaley . . ." Her eyes flicked to the back of the room, which made Bo feel like a spotlight was trained on him. He tried to look straight ahead and not at Mrs. Heard. ". . . ah . . . the base commander . . . has finally convinced the School Commission to visit Young Oaks next month. If you'll fill out this assessment of your room and the surrounding hallway, I can document the poor conditions here. I want the School Commission to see every last thing that is fixable, down to the smallest crack in the front sidewalk. Some of these things have needed repair since *you* were a student!"

Her gaze snapped back to Bo, as if he were a flashing sign.

"No classroom management issues?" she said.

"None yet," said Miss Loupe.

"Well, should you have any questions, I'm available." Her chuckle sounded like she was trying to start a stalled car.

After she left, Miss Loupe put the report on her desk. When they had finished the math pre-test, she carefully went over the remaining pages of the Student Handbook with them.

"Did you see they added pogo sticks because of me?" Bo whispered to Trey, pointing to the line about "Prohibited Modes of Transportation on School Grounds (Before or After Hours)."

Each student signed the bottom of page 26, stating that they did, indeed, understand that threats against the school were not a joking matter and that no weapons, even toys, could be on school property.

"What about jets?" Trey whispered to Bo, as he drew four F-15Es in formation at the top of page 12. They were releasing bombs onto the words below.

Next, Miss Loupe passed out the required reading list, plus the library's newsletter, *The Candy-Gram.*

"Look!" Zac said. "Miss Candy used my book review from this summer! *Al Capone Does My Shirts*. Page one!"

"Is that her real name?" Shaunelle said, peering at a blurry photo in the upper corner of the newsletter. It looked like the librarian was holding a bowl with gold marbles in it . . . but maybe that was candy?

At lunch, Miss Loupe chaperoned the class to the cafeteria, where she drank a diet soda and ate a prewrapped salad topped with six pale ribbons of ham and one hard-boiled egg cut into wedges, just like all the other teachers.

"Do you think she's going to act weird again this afternoon?" Melissa said at the girls' lunch table. "I don't know how we're supposed to learn anything if she keeps making us *guess* the answers!" She poked her plastic fork into her spaghetti noodles and twirled it around and around.

Allison unpacked her lunch of baby carrots and Oreo cookies. She handed one cookie to Aimee and one to Martina, keeping three for herself. She unscrewed a cookie top and delicately licked the white creamy filling.

"I don't know, but if you want to guess something, guess what you and Shaunelle are eating. That meat is, like, from yesterday's tacos."

Shaunelle quickly shook the noodles off her fork and picked up her slice of bread. Aimee and Martina nibbled their cookies next to Allison. Melissa popped a plump forkful of spaghetti meat into her mouth and chewed loudly.

At the boys' table, Trey was drawing a picture of Miss Loupe's bird tattoo on his napkin.

"No," said Rick. "The head was smaller, and the beak was longer . . . like a hummingbird. It definitely had its wings open." Sanjay nodded silently in agreement.

Bo took the pen from Trey and added tiny lines beside the outstretched wings to make them look as if they were beating quickly.

"I don't know anything more," said Rick. "I'm going to have to see it again."

After lunch, Miss Loupe handed out their social studies text-books, which, as Zac pointed out, were fatter than the local phone book and a lot more boring.

"You guys have fun *reading* about Germany," said Dillon. "I'll be living there! We get to go to Heidelberg Castle!" He didn't even bother signing his name inside the textbook cover.

Trey checked the inside of his worn textbook cover to see who had had it last year. No one he knew. No good doodles either. He set about fixing that.

Bo was still thinking about Zac's comment. "I wish these books had coupons in them. Like the ones in the phone book. You know, 'Free Hot Wings from Poppette's Pizza!' We could have 'Ten Percent Less Homework on Fridays!'"

"We don't have a phone book yet," Shaunelle said. "The rooms at the TLF are supposed to have one. Ours didn't."

Allison snorted, which made Aimee and Martina giggle. Shaunelle decided not to say that she read the phone book cover to cover whenever they moved to a new place. There wasn't much else to do at the Temporary Lodging Facility while her family waited for a base house.

"I wish we were still in the TLF," Melissa said, as she neatly wrote her full name on the inside cover. "We got to eat out every night. Now we only get to go to Hog Heaven when it's somebody's birthday."

Hog Heaven! Bo thought. He loved their famous basket of crispy hush puppies topped with spicy pork barbecue. It was the first place he and his family had eaten when the Air Force had moved them to Reform last year, and it made him think that this town, no matter how boring and small, at least had the food thing down right.

If he were in the Taped Space, how would he make someone guess that he was at Hog Heaven? That he was eating barbecue and not pizza? He could snort around like a pig, like he'd done for that killer *Charlotte's Web* book report he'd given in the fourth grade. No one here had seen that. That was one good thing about moving so much: You could reuse old work and no one ever knew.

What about those waitresses that worked there? The ones who could balance ten glasses of sweet tea on a tray and who brought you banana pudding when you were just *thinking* about spooning creamy, cookie-filled globs of it into your mouth? He didn't think he could pretend to be one of them, unless the game allowed you to talk. Then he could say, "What can I getcha, honey?" And "You wanna go whole hog on that?" which meant your barbecue sandwich came topped with a dab of tart, creamy coleslaw, and surrounded by hush puppies and three fistfuls of french fries.

How had Miss Loupe done it? How had she made them *believe*? And why wasn't she doing it today?

From their social studies texts, they read three firsthand accounts of the immigrant experience and discussed what it was like to adapt to new customs and rules. Then they moved on to science and reviewed lab safety. Forty-five minutes before school ended, Bo could stand it no longer. He tore off the back of his handbook and inked a thick rectangle to represent the Taped Space. In it, he wrote the words

Hey Trey.
Where am I?

He slid the note onto Trey's desk. Trey's pen skipped around the piece of paper, answering Bo's question with a drawing. When he passed the note back, there were Bo and Trey in combat gear, fending off a hissing cesspool.

Bo grinned. The Quagmire of Ignorance — it was back! Last year, their teacher, Mr. Nix, had spent the first week lecturing them about his favorite geometric figures. (*The octagon! Have you ever seen such perfection! Look at all those parallel sides!*) When Bo had yawned, Mr. Nix had pounced, quizzing Bo about the shape of the state flower of North Carolina.

"I just moved here," Bo had protested. "How would I know?"

Then he had asked Trey, who hadn't known either.

"Fine," Mr. Nix had warned, waving his freckled hands at the two of them. "Go ahead and sink into the Quagmire of Ignorance. The rest of us wish to set sail on the Sea of Knowledge."

Bo had oozed out of his seat and onto the floor with a series of loud *glub-glubs*. Mr. Nix then sailed him directly to the principal — his first visit. After that, it hadn't seemed to matter to Trey that his dad worked for Bo's dad. They were both in the Quagmire together.

This year, Mr. Nix was teaching first grade. Bo wondered if Allison's little brother, Tony, was in Mr. Nix's class, and if he was sinking or swimming. He added a kid's face to Trey's drawing, right in the sticky middle of the Quagmire. Two terrified eyes were barely visible above the creeping muck. A first-grade-sized hand waved desperately in the air. Bo wrote in a speech bubble: *Help! An octagon has my leg!*

Miss Loupe was suddenly standing next to his desk. Bo saw her shoes first. They were made of soft black leather, with an elastic strap over the foot. They looked like slippers and they hadn't made a sound as she approached. What had happened to her tennis shoes, the ones that were so new they squeaked, the ones he was positive had been on her feet minutes ago?

Miss Loupe eyed the Quagmire of Ignorance and the torn Handbook. Would she send him to the principal like Mr. Nix had?

Her finger tapped the words *WHERE AM I?* on his note.

"Would you and Trey help me, please?"

She turned and glided out the classroom door.

Bo bounced out of his desk, and he and Trey scrambled down the hall after Miss Loupe, who was walking quickly. They turned the corner seconds after she did.

There, blocking the way, was the ugliest couch Bo had ever seen. It was lumpy and green, and covered with fat gold-fringed pillows. It squatted on four brass legs and had bare spots on the arms and seat cushions, as if a fungus had eaten away the thick fuzz. It smelled faintly of stale tortilla chips.

"Quit staring," said the Ugly, Ugly Couch.

Or so Bo thought, until he saw Miss Loupe's head poking over the far end.

"Can you two handle this?"

Bo and Trey each grabbed an end of the ugly thing. It didn't feel as bad as it looked. The arms were soft, and they creaked slightly as the couch swayed between them down the hall. Miss Loupe preceded the couch, directing their every move as they tilted the beast through the doorway and into the room, which was loud with the voices of the rest of the class.

"Here," she instructed, pointing to a spot inside the Taped Space. "Line it up with the edge."

Bo and Trey thumped the couch down as the class spurted questions.

"Can I sit on it, Miss Loupe?"

"Is that yours?"

"What are we doing? Do we need a pencil for this?"

Miss Loupe motioned Bo and Trey back to their seats, then walked deliberately around the outside of the Taped Space to a spot in front of the chalkboard, where she toed her stealthy black slippers to the edge. The class quieted.

In the silence, she pushed her hands out in front of her, as if she were parting a heavy velvet curtain, and stepped, with careful grace, into the Taped Space.

She confronted the couch.

"I can smell your stench from here," she said to it. "Didn't you take a bath today?"

The class giggled nervously.

Suddenly, Miss Loupe grabbed a dingy pillow and whacked it against the arm of the Ugly, Ugly Couch.

"You reeky, onion-eyed nut-hook!" she shouted.

Bits of green fuzz burst into the air and floated before settling back onto the cushions. The class laughed, but even more awkwardly. What were they supposed to be thinking? Doing? Was Miss Loupe losing her mind before their eyes?

Bo, strangely, felt a twinge of pity for the couch. It wasn't its fault that it looked like a moldy block of partially shredded cheese.

Miss Loupe approached Melissa and offered her the pillow.

"Want to try it?" she asked.

"Is this for a grade?" Melissa said.

Miss Loupe withdrew the pillow. She turned to the couch, where she stretched herself out, as if to take a nap, with the pillow under her head and her feet crossed. She was so small that she only took up two of the three couch cushions.

"Ahhhhh," she said, sighing. "This is a most comfortable, cozy, and considerate couch." She patted the back of it affectionately. "Too bad that everyone thinks you're ugly."

Okay, Bo thought, *now I must be sinking into the Quagmire, because I have no idea what she's doing.*

"Too bad," Miss Loupe went on, "that everyone thinks *I'm* crazy. Too bad no one wants to join us. Too bad no one wants to sit upon the same couch that starred in *I Know When You're Alone.*"

"I saw that movie!" Allison said. "There's this girl, who keeps hearing this voice when she plays this music on this piano, but when she turns around, there's no one there, just this green . . . couch. Yeah, *this* couch, and then she finds this blood under the cushions and — *ewww*! Is there blood on that couch?"

"Special effects," said Miss Loupe. She sat up. "I got the couch from a friend of mine who worked at MiraGrand when I was in college in Los Angeles. I needed a couch for my apartment, and they were going to toss it, so I took it."

Now the whole class was staring in fascination at the couch, even if they'd never seen the movie.

Miss Loupe got up from the Ugly, Ugly Couch and moved behind it. She shoved the couch into the middle of the Taped Space so that it faced the class and stood behind it, her arms stretched out along its curved back.

"What happens when we place an object in the Taped Space?" she said. "Do we see it differently than if it were in the teachers' lounge or in a living room? What happens when someone talks to it? When I insulted it with my own weak language and then the bold words of Shakespeare? How did you feel when I hit the couch? Did you feel differently when I treated it kindly?"

Of course, thought Bo. *How could you not?* His hand twitched as if it wanted to rise into the air.

Wait. Maybe no one else had felt sorry for the couch. He wanted Miss Loupe to keep doing her crazy games, instead of real school, but he didn't want everyone to look at him like he was moldy shredded cheese either. He sat on his hand and glanced over at the window. It was sealed shut under rippled coats of yellowed paint. He wished Miss Loupe could push it open a tiny crack.

Miss Loupe was moving on. "Let's try it with another object. Rick, may I borrow your ID card?"

Rick handed over the tan laminated card.

"What can we do with *this?*" said Miss Loupe. She waved the ID card. "And *this?*" She patted the couch.

No one knew.

"You're right. We need one more thing. Would someone come sit on the couch, please?" She looked at the class expectantly.

This time, Bo couldn't help it. His hand rose into the air.

"Yes, Bo, come on up."

Bo made his way to the front of the class. As he crossed the edge of the Taped Space, he deliberately tripped over the flat, beige strip of tape and sent himself rocketing into the cushions of the Ugly, Ugly Couch. The class laughed, and he wondered for a second if Miss Loupe had any rules about how to treat her couch. She had whacked it, but . . . He turned around and sat up.

Miss Loupe didn't say a thing. She began to take his picture, only she used the ID card instead of a real camera. Her fingers gripped the rectangular edges of the card as she lifted it to her face and squeezed one eye shut. She peeked around the card with the other eye, regarding him intently. Then she advanced on the couch, rotating her imaginary camera from side to side, searching for the best angle.

The whole class was looking at Bo as if he should be doing something in response. Trey had overlapped his hands so they formed a line in front of his neck and was slowly raising the Quagmire over his chin and mouth and nose, his lips *glub-glubb*ing silently.

He wasn't going to sink, thought Bo. It couldn't be that hard. He slicked down his hair and pasted a fake grin on his face. He beamed from the lobe of one freckled ear to the other. He twinkled his eyes, one at a time. He shook his head as if dazed from the repeated flash and waved to his legions of scream-ing fans.

"Trey! Good to see you, man! Zac! Check it out! I'm a rock star! Yo, Melissa! Want to interview me?"

But inside, he was wondering: What did Miss Loupe want him to do? Was this right?

He began to bounce on the couch. It felt like a trampoline. Could he launch himself over the side?

Now Miss Loupe was acting as if there was something wrong with her camera, shaking it and repeatedly looking through the imaginary viewfinder at him, and then taking her eye away and surveying him and the Ugly, Ugly Couch. It was as if she was trying to tell him something. Should he get up? Leave the couch and take the camera from her?

Then, suddenly, Miss Loupe had stopped taking pictures of him. Her imaginary camera transformed back into an ID card, which she handed to Bo. "Here you are, sir. It looks *exactly like you.*"

Bo did the only thing he could think of. He took one look at Rick's picture, did a double take, and passed out. He flopped his head over the arm of the Ugly, Ugly Couch and let his tongue loll uselessly from his mouth. His toes twitched in a last shudder of consciousness.

The whole class, except Rick, broke out laughing, and Bo stretched his tongue out a millimeter more, completing his lifeless pose.

"Well," Miss Loupe said, looking down at his limp body, "that's one way to end a scene." She turned to address the class. "As a general rule, you should try not to pass out or die. It gives your partner nothing, absolutely nothing, to work with."

Bo recovered his extended tongue, which was making him leak drool onto the couch cushions. He opened his eyes and tried to look as alive as possible.

"The best thing to do," Miss Loupe went on, "is to say, 'Yes, *and* . . .'"

She handed Rick back his card, which he stuffed into his pocket without looking at it. She motioned for Bo to return to his seat.

Yes? Hadn't he said yes? thought Bo. He trudged to the back row, sat down, and stuck both hands under his legs.

"That means you add new information to the scene. I should have explained it better before we began. Think of it like cooking: What new flavor can you throw into the pot that will go with the rest of the ingredients but make it somehow different, somehow better?

"Let me give you an example," Miss Loupe said. She walked over to her desk and turned a picture frame around.

"This is my brother Marc," she said. The man in the picture had close-cropped hair and a wicked grin. He looked like Miss Loupe, minus the earrings. "He's two years older than I am, and he's in Afghanistan with a Special Forces team right now."

"He's cute," said Allison.

"Warriors aren't cute," said Trey.

"We can't talk much," said Miss Loupe, "but we e-mail each other as often as we can. I promised to tell him about my adventures here with you, and he promised to tell me about his adventures there. Except that there are things he's not allowed to write in an e-mail — things that might endanger a mission. So sometimes we play games in our e-mails instead. He gives me a line of a story, and then I give him one, and we try to keep it going for as long as we can."

She lifted a piece of paper from her desk and held it up. "Yesterday he sent me a new one and dared me to try it with all of you." She read the e-mail out loud:

"So, Room 208, I hear you have my baby sister as your teacher. Did she tell you about the time I taught her how to tie her shoes wrong? She came home from kindergarten and punched me."

The class laughed.

"But unlike me, she's good at teaching things. You'll see. Have you learned the 'Yes, and . . .' game yet? If you have, here's a line for you."

Miss Loupe picked up the picture of Marc and acted as if he were saying the words: "The students of Room 208 were walking in the mountains of Afghanistan when they met a huge, three-eyed, double-jawed, dirty-furred, snarling monster. . . ."

She pointed the picture frame at Kylie. "What should I tell him happens next?"

"We run away!" said Kylie.

"Well, yes," said Miss Loupe. "Wouldn't we all? But for the sake of this game, let's see what happens if the rule is: You *can't* run away. Then what?" She pointed at Kylie again, prompting her: "Yes, and . . ."

"Yes, and . . . we looked around for a cave to hide in!"

"Good!" said Miss Loupe. "Yes, but we couldn't find one and it was getting dark. . . ." She pointed to Zac.

"Yes, and my pants fell down. . . ." The boys laughed, but the girls looked disgusted. Miss Loupe pointed at Aimee.

"Yes, and your underwear glowed in the dark. . . ."

Miss Loupe grinned. She pointed at Martina.

"Yes, and the monster said you looked like a humongous marshmallow. . . ."

"Yes, and he built a roaring fire. . . ." added Miss Loupe.

"Yes, and I wanted to run away, but I couldn't," said Melissa, "so I went to the river and jumped in to make myself all wet —"

Allison interrupted. "I don't get it. Why are we talking about monsters? And Bo was acting stupid up there. Like, I had no idea where you were."

Bo's mouth opened. "We were ON STAGE!" he yelled.

The whole class turned around to look at him, but Miss Loupe flashed him a huge smile.

"Yes!" she said. "When we're on stage, we can be anywhere. We can see what happens next when we don't run from monsters. And if we say yes, we can take *ugly* or *stupid* and turn it into a new picture altogether."

She put the frame back on her desk. "I can't wait to tell Marc he'd better send us another first line, because all of you *aced* that one!"

The bell rang, and the second day of school was over. Miss Loupe reminded them about their math homework for the next day. The class shoved pencils and books into their backpacks and lined up at the door.

What happens next?

What happens next?

What happens next?

Bo left Room 208, but he felt the possibilities bouncing around his brain, like golf balls launched off chunks of concrete.

6
ALL THE TIME

"I'm not going to North Carolina." Gari trailed her mom down the hallway, talking steadily to her mom's back, as if it weren't moving away from her. "I have it all worked out. I can stay here, and you won't have to worry because I'll be —"

Her mom stopped at the end of the hallway and looked up at a cord dangling from the ceiling.

"— staying with Tandi," finished Gari.

Gari's mom yanked at the cord. A set of attic stairs unfolded, creaking and popping. The springs that held them together swayed like they were going to break.

"Tandi isn't family. I want you to be with family while I'm gone."

"Maybe I could stay with Tandi until . . . you know . . . until the Army or somebody could find . . . could find . . . I mean, I do have other family . . . if we knew where —"

"No," her mom said. She shook the stairs to make sure they were locked in place. Little puffs of dust clouded the air. "If your dad was going to show up, he would have done it by now. It's always been you and me. Always."

Gari watched the dust drift down and pushed her glasses tightly against her nose. "But I could . . ."

Her mom put a foot on the stairs. "No. The Army's only giving me three weeks to get ready, and we have enough to do without arguing over this."

Gari discovered that she was biting her lower lip so hard that she had torn the skin. She wasn't arguing. She was proposing a different plan. What was wrong with that?

But her mom ended the discussion, reaching out and hooking one of her fingers around one of Gari's.

"All the time," she said, and the familiar words, like the beginning of a song, called up the response from Gari.

"Love you all the time too, Mom," she answered. She did. Just not so much at this exact moment. She slid her finger out of her mom's grasp.

Her mom climbed up, and her head and shoulders disappeared into the attic.

"Here's my old trumpet," her mom called, her voice muffled. "You can take that with you, if you want. Maybe you can try . . ." She went on talking, even though her head went farther up inside the attic and Gari couldn't hear her words anymore.

Gari stood at the bottom of the stairs, looking at her mom's feet.

There had to be a better plan. There had to.

7
FOLLOW ME

Over the next several days, Miss Loupe had the class transfer her mysterious quotes about frames, art, and saying yes to strips of shiny white poster board, which they mounted with blue putty to the pitted and scarred cinder block walls of their classroom.

"Say yes?" said Melissa, as she struggled to get the poster board to hang straight. "What happened to 'Just say no'?"

"You should have hit the couch when she said you could," said Bo. "Why did you say no?"

"I couldn't help it," Melissa said. "I never can tell what she's thinking. Sometimes she teaches like a normal teacher, and then . . . WHAM!"

"It's her shoes, dummy," said Allison. "My mom says a person's shoes are important, and if you paid attention to clothes, you would know that." She bumped her name-brand tennis shoe against Melissa's plain white one.

It was true. Miss Loupe did teach them sixth-grade math and science and social studies and English. But every afternoon, for at least a few minutes, she kicked off her regular footwear and slipped on her black stealth shoes. What happened after that was anybody's guess.

One afternoon she began with:

"Give me the name of an object."

"A boat!" yelled Zac.

"A place?" said Miss Loupe.

"On the couch!" said Melissa.

"*That's* kind of boring," said Bo.

"An event?" continued Miss Loupe.

"PT!" yelled Martina.

"What's PT?" whispered Kylie to Shaunelle. She knew some military stuff, like PCS (Permanent Change of Station), because her mom was fluent in the language of selling houses to everyone who moved in and out. But some things still puzzled her.

"Physical training," Shaunelle whispered back. "Like P.E., except for grown-ups. You have to —"

She gasped, because Miss Loupe had jumped up on the Ugly, Ugly Couch. She was perched on its flat, squat back, one leg hanging over each side. And then she started rowing. And *singing.*

"When my great-granny was ninety-one," she belted out, pulling with all her might against imaginary oars, "she did PT just for fun!"

Martina giggled. She knew this jody call. Her mom sang it while she shined her boots. Then her dad would tease her mom and say, "Hey, aren't YOU going to be ninety-one when you finally retire?"

"When my great-granny was ninety-two," Miss Loupe bellowed, "she did PT better than you!"

She looked sideways at her class, continuing to row, and pretended to wipe sweat from her brow. "Come on, I'm fading out here all alone!"

The class laughed. But they didn't sing or row. They watched.

"When my great-granny was ninety-three," Miss Loupe sang, more weakly now. She paused, her oars trailing as if she were faltering in the water. She listed to one side of the couch. She looked like she might pass out or die.

But that would end it! thought Bo. Didn't she just tell him the other day not to do that?

"She did PT better than me!" he called out.

Miss Loupe gave a whoop of delight and righted herself on the couch.

"You! Let's go!" she said to Bo. "On the boat!"

Bo hustled to the front of the room. He kicked off his shoes and scrambled up the cushions onto the top of the couch. He'd done lots of rowing on the lake near his grandparents' house in Tennessee. He mimed spitting into each hand, then grabbed for the oars, pulling in tandem with Miss Loupe.

"Who's next?" said Miss Loupe. "We need more crew!"

Bo yelled, "When my great-granny was ninety-four . . ."

He pointed his imaginary oar at Trey.

"She ran two miles and ran ten more!" said Trey.

Trey ran to climb aboard next to Bo.

"When my great-granny was ninety-five . . ." Trey chanted.

"She did PT to stay alive!" Zac yelled, racing for the couch.

"When my great-granny was ninety-six . . ."

"She did PT backward just for kicks," called Kylie, before another boy could yell out. She tucked herself in between Miss Loupe and Bo.

Soon the whole boat crew was chanting in unison, as rhymes flew back and forth between the boat and the shore:

"When my great-granny was ninety-seven . . ."

"She up and died, she went to heaven!"

"When my great-granny was ninety-eight . . ."

"She met St. Peter at the Pearly Gate!"

Miss Loupe hopped off the couch and went off on a riff:

"St. Peter, St. Peter, sorry I'm late!"

She lifted up her hands in apology. Then she took a giant step to the left, turned and faced where she had been standing, and stroked an imaginary beard.

"St. Peter said, with a toothy grin . . ."

Miss Loupe paused for effect and then snapped out:

"Drop down, Granny, and give me ten!"

With a giant step to the right, she was back to being the great-granny. She did ten quick push-ups without even breathing hard.

Then she stood up and applauded her crew on the Ugly, Ugly Couch.

"You see? We got into a rhythm of passing the lead back and forth, and it got easier and easier as we went along!"

"You're good at push-ups!" said Melissa. "You could be in the military!"

"Well," said Miss Loupe, "I was once a cadet at the Air Force Academy."

"You were in the Air Force?" said Bo. He tried to imagine her in uniform, with no earrings or belly ring, standing motionless in formation.

"No," she said. Her eyes went to Marc's picture for a brief moment. "I left after my freshman year."

The bell for the end of the day rang, and all the rowers scrambled off the couch to get their backpacks.

"Spelling test tomorrow!" Miss Loupe called after them. "Study your words! Try making a jody call with them!"

The next afternoon, after the spelling test, she donned her soft black shoes and pulled an old hooded sweatshirt from her desk drawer.

"The sweatshirt is one *object*," she said. "A WHAT. Can someone give me a WHERE?"

"Someone left it," said Allison. "At the wrong house."

"Yes, and . . ." said Miss Loupe. "Can someone give me SOMETHING THAT HAPPENS?"

"When they came back to get it, a cat was sleeping on it," said Bo.

"Yes, and when I wrestled the cat," said Trey, "one of the ties tore off. . . ."

"Yes, and the cat swallowed it. . . ." said Aimee.

"Yes, and we had to take her to the vet. . . ." said Shaunelle.

"Yes, and we had a wreck on the way and the cat escaped. . . ." said Rick.

"Good," said Miss Loupe. "Now let's try to put our *object*, our *place*, and our *event* into action."

She called Rick and Shaunelle up into the Taped Space. Rick was the cat, curled on top of the sweatshirt. Shaunelle approached him and tried to tug the sweatshirt away. Rick wouldn't budge. She tugged harder. Rick didn't give an inch. Shaunelle yanked with all her might, and there was a loud *r — iiii — p!* A pencil-sized gap appeared in the seam of the sweatshirt.

"OH!" said Shaunelle. "I didn't mean for that to happen!"

"I think I can fix that," said Miss Loupe. "But what do you think went wrong here?"

"Rick wouldn't move!" said Shaunelle.

"Cats don't move unless they want to," said Rick. "Mine doesn't."

"Ah," said Miss Loupe. "You're both right. So how do you move forward when both of you are right?"

"Take turns?" offered Shaunelle, thinking of the arguments she'd refereed between her younger sisters.

"Exactly," said Miss Loupe. "One person leads, the other follows. It's like a good stage fight."

"Fight?" said Bo and Trey together.

Miss Loupe regarded them with a half-smile. "I don't think I should've mentioned that. I should've said, one person leads, the other person follows . . . like good ballroom dancing."

The two boys fell back in their seats. Miss Loupe picked up the sweatshirt from the arm of the couch.

"Isn't that an Academy sweatshirt?" asked Allison.

"Yes, it is," said Miss Loupe.

"Why didn't you stay at the Academy, ma'am?" said Melissa. "Because you wanted to be a teacher?"

"That's a story that takes more time than we have," said Miss Loupe, eyeing the clock at the back of the room. She exchanged her slip-ons for laced-up tennis shoes. "I have bus duty today."

"So do I!" said Kylie. She got out her Safety Patrol sash.

Melissa still had her notebook open.

"Can't we do more writing?" she said. "I'm not too good at . . . at . . ." She gestured toward the Taped Space.

"We'll do a fiction and poetry unit later in the year," Miss Loupe told her. "In the meantime, thinking about WHAT, WHERE, and WHAT HAPPENS can help you write scenes. And WHO," she added. "Characters are very important."

Melissa nodded and closed her notebook.

Bo shook his head. Why did Melissa want to write things when they could be DOING them?

Later that night, at 9:58, Bo lay awake, listening to the sound of his dad's flight suits tumbling in the dryer. He leaned out of his bed and shoved the window open a crack, so he could hear the music that marked the official end of the military day.

In the morning, at six A.M., the song was Reveille — *Dut-dut-dutta-dah! Dut-dut-dutta-dah!* — which meant "Wake up!" At noon, "The Air Force Song" rang out across the base:

Off we go into the wild blue yonder,
Climbing high into the sun!

At four thirty, the speakers played the national anthem for the Retreat Ceremony. Then at ten o'clock, like tonight, the music of

Taps floated over the night air. Taps was much slower than Reveille.

Dun-dun-daaaah. Dun-dun-daaaah.

Solemn and steady, the song drew out its notes as if trying to linger far beyond the end of this particular day.

Sometimes when Bo heard it, he counted back in his head, walking through each house he'd lived in that he could remember. In each house, he'd had a different key, but the same tag attached to it. It was a strip of bright red cloth with the words REMOVE BEFORE FLIGHT on it in white letters — bright red so Bo wouldn't lose it. His dad had shown him the much larger, real tags on the covers for fragile jet parts.

He wondered how many houses from now he would be thinking back to this room, to this house, to this town, and know that everyone here had mostly forgotten who Bo Whaley was. It was eerie, like thinking about himself in a long hall of mirrors, each one smaller than the last.

Bo pushed his window shut again. Now that the flight suit zippers had stopped clunking against the dryer, he could hear his parents' voices. They were discussing Gari, legal paperwork, and how to turn his dad's office into a bedroom.

Boring. Boring. Boring.

He fell asleep imagining that he and Trey were dueling, like fighter jets in a dogfight, on the backs of very ugly, but surprisingly maneuverable, couches.

The next day, he came early to class. Room 208 was empty except for Miss Loupe, who was sitting at her computer, checking her e-mail. Bo caught a glimpse of a photo of rugged mountains and a military vehicle with dust flying up around it. How should he ask her so she would say yes?

Miss Loupe turned to greet him.

"Hey there," she said. "Here for your ballroom dance lesson? Rumba or tango today? Your choice."

She laughed at his horrified face.

"Come on, Bo. Even Marc knows how to dance a little bit. It's good for impressing the girls."

"Is that him?" said Bo, leaning in to the computer.

"Yes. Although I hardly recognize him under that bushy beard." Miss Loupe moved to the side so Bo could see the screen. "His team grows beards so they can blend in with the local culture when they need to." She regarded him curiously. "Do you think you'll join the military one day?"

"My dad thinks I will," said Bo. He stared at Marc in his uniform and his reflective sunglasses. Then he took a breath and jumped into the reason he'd come early.

"Yesterday, you said we could do stage fighting. . . ." He shifted his backpack to the floor.

Miss Loupe rubbed at her hair with one hand, making it stand up even spikier. "I knew you wouldn't let me get away with dropping that," she said.

Bo waited.

"Stage fighting is an advanced technique. Lots of leading and following. We might learn it if I get the gr —" She stopped.

"Get the what?"

"Sorry," said Miss Loupe. "Top secret for now." She pivoted

on her chair and closed out her e-mail program. Then she looked back at him. "Can I trust you?" she said.

Bo felt his throat dry up. *Yes,* he wanted to say. *Yes, you can trust me!* But he wasn't quite sure what would be required.

Miss Loupe stood up. "If I can, then I could show you how to fall."

"Fall?" said Bo. "I know how to do that!"

"Not this way, you don't."

She came out from behind her desk into the Taped Space.

"Falling is important to fight safety," she said. "The last thing you want is to thud to the floor uncontrollably. Let me show you."

She readied herself, and then stumbled backward as if she'd been punched. Her legs buckled under her, and she collapsed sideways to the floor in one graceful motion, with hardly a sound.

She stood up again. "It all comes from your core," she said, making a fist just in front of her lower stomach. "If you're strong here, then all your limbs move together and in control." She grinned. "I hate to say it again, but it really helps if you take dance like I did."

She pulled some cushions off the Ugly, Ugly Couch onto the floor.

"Try it here first," said Miss Loupe. "For a guaranteed soft landing."

Bo tried it, diving backward into the cushions, making them skid in two directions.

"Not like you've been launched from a cannon," said Miss Loupe. "A *controlled* landing."

Bo tried it again, more slowly. THUD! Still wrong.

He closed his eyes and replayed Miss Loupe's fall in his head in slow motion. There was the SMASH! when she was punched. Like glass breaking in a window. There was the stumble backward. OOF! Then there was . . . YES! He saw it! Her knees folded, her arms went limp, her neck was loose, but there right in the middle of her body was the engine, like the power that held up the jets as they hovered above the runway before touching down.

Or the way Taps seemed to hang in the air.

Or the way he felt at the top of a bounce on his pogo stick.

Weightless. Powerful.

He crumpled, each part of his body almost rolling down onto the cushions: First the side of his ankles touched, then his bent knees, the edge of his butt, his right arm, then the back of both shoulders as he flattened out and sank to the floor. SWOOSH! The cushions stayed in place this time.

Miss Loupe nodded. "Now somersaults."

"What?" Surely she knew that Mrs. Heard had suspended him for somersaulting last year.

"Somersaults," said Miss Loupe. "I can't show you anything else unless you do."

Bo hopped up. He looked at the clock. "Can't you show me at least one fight move?"

Miss Loupe's hand made tight circles in the air. "Show me."

Bo did. He somersaulted three times. No problems there.

Miss Loupe looked at the clock then too. "Something short," she said. She moved so they both stood at one end of the cushions on the floor. "This is something I showed Marc the first time he visited me in L.A., when I was in drama school. Surprised the heck out of him that I could do it! The choreography goes: slow, slow, quick, quick, slow. Or: one . . . two. One, two . . . THREE!"

"Like counting in jody calls?" Bo guessed.

"Not exactly. Choreography involves instructions for your body, not your voice." She looked directly at him, her gaze steady. "One," she said. "Slow. We make eye contact. That ensures both of us are ready to begin, so no one gets hurt."

Usually, Bo avoided a teacher's direct stare. He lifted his eyebrows and widened his eyes to signal that he was, indeed, making contact. If he were doing this with Trey, he would have rolled his eyes back in his head and Trey would've snorted.

"Two," she said. "Again, slow. Pull your fist back."

Bo balled his hand and drew it back. "Like this?"

"Make it bigger," Miss Loupe coached. "You want the audience to see the motion."

Bo exaggerated his windup, sweeping his arm slowly back into the air.

"Next part," said Miss Loupe. "This is quick! One: You swing; I block at the same time."

He swung, and she stopped his fist with her hand.

"Good," she said. She swiftly bent one knee and grabbed Bo's leg near his ankle. "Two. Gotcha!"

She looked up at him. "Now THREE! The big, slow finale! Over you go."

"What?"

"Drop over my back and somersault onto the cushions," said Miss Loupe. "As you go, I'll throw my hand up like I'm flipping you by your leg."

Bo eyed the cushions, which were lined up behind her like a bumpy runway.

She straightened up. "It's easier with momentum," she said. "Let's try it from the top."

One. They made eye contact.

Two. He made a big show of pulling back his arm.

One. He punched. She blocked.

Two. She reached for his leg and . . .

"GO!" she said.

Whomp! He flipped right over her and onto the cushions in a puff of green fuzz. He threw out his arms as if he'd had the wind knocked out of him.

"THREE!" said Bo. "I was leading then, right?" He flopped over onto his stomach and then scrambled to his feet, ready to go at it again.

"Right," said Miss Loupe. "To the audience, it looks like I'm flipping you, but you did the work." She smiled. "You also did the tango." She shuffled her feet in a rhythm: slow, slow, quick, quick, slow. Slow, slow, quick, quick, slow.

Bo laughed. Like he would ever be caught doing *that.*

Miss Loupe made direct eye contact with him once more. "You have to promise me you won't do this at recess or anywhere else in school," she said. "Only here, with supervision."

How had she known what his recess plans were?

"You can trust me," said Bo.

They tucked the cushions back onto the Ugly, Ugly Couch. He'd have to show Trey the flipping part at home after school. But maybe this afternoon, when Miss Loupe put on her stage shoes, he could take the lead again.

8

MEANWHILE

Gari's mom had to get new uniforms and new boots. None of her old ones from the attic fit. Even if they had, they weren't the right color anymore. The Army had switched from a black and dark green print to a digitized camouflage of sandy brown, gray, and light green. Gari thought it looked like the washed-out blur they put over someone's face on TV when they didn't want you to be able to identify them. That was the point of camouflage, she supposed, to stay hidden, but why did it have to be so ugly?

Gari's mom wore her uniform when the two of them went into the front office of Seattle Junior Academy and explained their situation. They asked for Gari's application fee back.

Gari remembered what she'd written on her application:

I like math and English, but my best talent is probably art. One day, I want my art to make big statements, about things that matter. I want to get started on these plans right away at Seattle Junior Academy.

She hadn't mentioned that she didn't know how to do that yet, exactly. She had lots of ideas, but so far, the only "big" thing she'd tried to plan was Tandi's campaign. And now, that might never happen.

The secretary said the application fee was nonrefundable, but maybe, in this case . . . well, she'd have to check. She apologized. "We don't have any other parents in the military." At least, she didn't think so.

Next, they went to see a lawyer about guardianship papers. He made multiple copies of everything.

Gari sat in a nearby chair and poked her straw around the bottom chunks of ice in the tall cup of orange soda her mom had bought for her.

Then he asked about their finances. More copies. He asked about their house. Their car. More copies.

Gari fiddled with the straw wrapper, making a loop with one long end and one short. Then she folded it, by wrapping the strips back and forth around each other, into a tiny, flat, five-pointed shape. She used her fingernail to push a dent in each side, lifting the edges and shaping it into a 3-D star. There was a store near Seattle Junior Academy that sold colorful strips of paper in plastic tubes, just for making these stars. But a straw wrapper worked.

I need hundreds of these for Tandi's campaign. We can make a trail of them, from the front door to the lunchroom. When everyone gets to the cafeteria, we'll dim the lights, the posters will glow, and we'll wow them all.

Could Tandi carry that off without her? She doubted it. Tandi thought you told people what to do, like vote for you, and they did it. But it was harder than that. You had to see something in your head before you could make it happen. It didn't even matter if what you saw or what you made didn't last, like the glowy lights or the paper stars; it was how people thought about it, and you, afterward that counted.

She dropped the star into the few drops of soda in the bottom of her paper cup. It transformed instantly into a bit of mushy paper. But she had already gotten what she needed from that one star. She would tell Tandi, and they would start folding paper stars tonight. She wasn't giving up. Not yet.

If only she could see a plan in her head that would make her mom change her mind. What if she could think of something to tell this lawyer, something horrible she'd done that would make it impossible for her mom to leave her?

No, that would make her mom mad. Gari hadn't done anything horrible anyway. Only imagined the entire U.S. Army computer system crashing and losing every record that her mom even existed. Only shot a dirty look at that recruiter in the mall. Only flipped through that book in the library about diseases, trying to come up with one she could fake.

She heard the lawyer asking about a will. Lots and lots of signing and copies followed that.

After they left the lawyer's office, they drove home. It was strange to be out with her mom in the middle of the day during the week. Her mom worked from an office inside their house, supervising her home health-care business, but she was usually too swamped with calls and paperwork and client referrals to go out much during the day, unless it was to meet a new patient or follow up on a complaint. What was going to happen to the nurses who worked for her? Would she have any clients left when she got back?

"Mom, you won't actually be *in* the war, will you?" said Gari. She and her mom had watched old World War II movies last year around Veterans Day. She knew this war was nothing like that. On the TV and in the newspaper, it was all about ambushes and roadside bombs and rocket attacks. And who was the enemy? Didn't they look just like the Iraqi people her mom would be helping?

Her mom pulled into their driveway. "Everywhere in Iraq is a war zone, at least on paper. I'll get hazardous-duty pay." She unbuckled her seat belt, but she stayed in the car with Gari. "But no, I'll be on a secure American base, away from most of the violence, taking care of wounded soldiers and airmen, and probably some injured Iraqis too. We're the first stop, and then critical patients are flown back to the States for long-term rehab." She picked up the folder of legal paperwork. "I'll be safe."

Gari wasn't so sure. In the newspaper that morning, she'd seen a picture of an antiwar rally downtown. The people holding signs in the photograph had fake blood streaked on their faces. They had poured buckets of red paint on the sidewalk. And some of them were lying down in the street, their arms and legs as stiff as if they were dead.

A war was a war, wasn't it? And her mom would be right in it.

9

THE CRACK IN EVERYTHING

Room 208 began another week of school. Pledge. Announcements. Homework collected. Melissa began a schedule of who had had a turn in the Taped Space and who had not. Allison debuted a new pair of navy-blue shoes with tiny heels. Bo asked what they would be doing at the end of the day. Miss Loupe said, as always, "Wait and see." They had just opened their math books when the librarian stopped by.

"Green Eggs and Ham!" she swore in mock astonishment at the sight of the Ugly, Ugly Couch. There was a touch of sawdust in her loosely curled hair, which was barely contained by a striped scarf, and a splotch of gray paint on the light brown skin above her left elbow.

"Sorry to bother you," Miss Candy said, still staring at the couch, "but do you still want your students to be Reading Buddies for a first-grade class?"

"Of course," Miss Loupe replied.

"Good. I've got you paired with Mr. Nix. I was going to wait until next month, but he's breathing down my neck!"

She stroked the arm of the Ugly, Ugly Couch.

"I guess you're using this?" she said. "It would look great

tucked under the Reading Castle I'm building. Have you seen it? I could cover this with some purple fabric and . . ."

"Sorry, I have further plans for it," Miss Loupe said. "But we'll be glad to invite our Buddies to come read on it one day."

"Good," Miss Candy said. "They'll like that. I'm starting a book club, if any of you want to join. Details will be in the next issue of *The Candy-Gram*!"

She popped out the door. Then she stuck her head back in.

"Have you started your report yet?" she said to Miss Loupe.

Miss Loupe shook her head. She patted the large stack of paper. "My class is going to help me this week."

Miss Candy nodded and left. After the door closed behind her, Miss Loupe put down her math book and reached into her desk drawer. She brought out another picture frame.

"Remember how I told you that I dropped out of the Academy? Well, that makes me the only person in my family not in the military."

As she talked, she let them pass the second frame around the room.

"My older sister flies C-130s for the Air Force. She's stationed in Japan. My younger brother is in his third year at the Air Force Academy. And as I told you, Marc joined the Army Special Forces. He's been in Afghanistan, near Kandahar, for several months now."

As each member of Room 208 held the frame, they could see that it held a handwritten quote on lined notebook paper. They could also see that there was a long crack in the glass, from edge to edge.

The words said:

> *There is a crack, a crack in everything.*
> *That's how the light gets in.*

"It's from a song," Miss Loupe explained. "One of Marc's favorites. He sent this to me after I left the Academy and moved to California. He says the glass wasn't cracked when he mailed it, but I think it was." She smiled. "He also swears he didn't let my cat, Nachos, eat a whole bottle of salsa during the Super Bowl, but that stain on the couch says he did."

The frame had made it to the back row, where Trey was studying it.

"But why?" asked Allison. "Why did he send it?"

"I guess you could say that my dropping out of the Academy caused a crack in my family," said Miss Loupe. "Mostly with my dad. I didn't want that to happen, but it did. Marc was trying to tell me that cracks are painful, but they can bring good things too."

Allison looked at Marc's picture on Miss Loupe's desk. *Cute* and *nice*, she thought.

Miss Loupe drew a flat, teardrop-shaped brass object from the neck of her canary-yellow shirt. It was attached to a slender chain.

"Marc also sent me this. Does anyone know what it is?" No one said anything. "My name, Loupe, is a French word that means 'imperfect gem.' This —"

She pressed her fingernail into a notch on the teardrop, causing a glass oval to swing out from inside the brass casing on a tiny hinge.

"This is also a loupe. 'Loupe, with a little l,' Marc calls it. It's a special magnifying glass for detecting imperfections."

She walked back to Bo, who had just taken the frame from Trey. She placed the lens in front of his eye. "Look at Marc's note. What do you see?"

Bo hesitated. "Black lines?"

"Yes, that's the pen ink. What else?"

"String? Or hair or something . . ."

"Those are the tiny fibers that hold the paper together. An expert could tell you from those fibers exactly where the paper was made. Isn't it amazing how much information you can get from something so ordinary?"

She took the frame from Bo and walked back to the front. "What other writing could we look at?"

Zac offered the last issue of *The Candy-Gram*, the one with his review in it.

"Dots!" he said when Miss Loupe placed her loupe over his words.

"Yes, because computer printers, unlike felt pens, shoot out hundreds of tiny jets of ink."

"Like when they do tattoos on TV," Rick said. "Can we look at yours with the loupe?"

"I don't think that will be necessary," Miss Loupe said, closing the lens. "But the point is that nothing is ordinary if you examine it closely. And the things that make someone imperfect are also the things that make them who they are. That's one thing I learned at drama school: how to use small things to make an audience see me in a new way."

She sat down on the couch, crossed her legs, and held her back stiff and her hands folded in her lap.

"Am I a proper young lady who is meeting her future in-laws for the first time?"

She flipped to lie on her back with one hand over her belly. "Or an old woman who has eaten too much pie?"

She curled up on one arm and licked her paws. "Or a very spoiled cat?

"It's all in how I make you look at me, isn't it?"

She got up from the couch and pulled a large box from behind her desk. She pushed it into the middle of the Taped Space.

"Marc asked for little toys and school or health supplies that he and his buddies can give to the kids in Afghanistan. If you want to help, you can drop your ordinary things into this box. I promise you those kids need a new way of seeing us." She placed a pack of lined paper and a package of felt-tipped pens into the box. "This is what I'm sending."

She smiled. "And while you're looking at things in a new way, if you notice a crack, would you please let me know for the report? You may borrow my loupe if you like."

She placed the framed quote next to Marc's picture, and they returned to the math lesson, but just like that, the class started finding cracks everywhere.

Allison noticed a crack while checking her hair in the mirror in the girls' bathroom. Why did that crack have to be in the middle, where it divided her face into two parts? It made her feel like when her dad fought with her mom over who got to see her when. She brought in two sets of hair ribbons for the box.

Martina found the same crack, but she liked it. What if everybody could see both halves of her, Filipino and white, instead of one or the other, all the time? She smiled at herself in the mirror and stared at the place where her two mouths came together. She brought in some toothpaste.

Dillon thought about the three huge moving crates his family had shipped out to Germany. Hundreds of his LEGOs were squeezed in there, along with his mom's green-and-white china, his dad's half-rebuilt motorcycle, and his sister's piles of comics. What if the boat delivering the crates developed a crack? He took his ruler and rubbed at the groove in the side of his desk, making it millimeters deeper. He brought in a large bottle of glue.

Trey drew a map of Afghanistan based on the one in his social studies book. When he got home, he crumpled up the paper and stuffed it into a glass of iced tea that his mom had left on the counter. After it dried, he carefully opened the map and admired the yellowed "old" cracks in his authentic-looking document. He thought about next spring, when his dad would deploy again to the Middle East. He brought in a set of colored pencils.

Melissa politely pointed out a crack in the lunchroom cash register to Mrs. Purdy, the cafeteria manager.

"Do you see this crack here, ma'am?" she asked. "It might affect your work."

Mrs. Purdy's hot-pink fingernails stopped tapping the register's keys. She peered at the crack, which ran all the way up the side of the dull gray machine. "Oh, honey, don't fret about that. This machine's older than Jesus."

She tucked back a tight gray curl that had escaped from her hairnet, smiled warmly at Melissa, and resumed ringing up her lunch. Afterward, though, she ran her hand over the side of the register and frowned.

Melissa brought in several packages of crackers. As she carefully tucked them into the box, she wondered if Marc would get her joke.

Shaunelle found a crack in the back of her favorite bookcase that weekend when her family left the TLF and settled into their three-bedroom base house. She smiled as she covered the crack with her collection of mysteries. She didn't have to share a room with her sisters anymore, so no one would tell on her if she stayed up all night reading. She could invite Aimee and Martina over. Without Allison. She brought in a mini-flashlight with batteries.

Bo wasn't sure how great cracks were. Or mistakes. He had a golf ball he had found near the driving range that was stamped on one side with a picture of an F-15E. On the other side were the words

There are no mulligans in combat

Which meant, basically, "Don't mess up, or you'll die."

Bo knew there was one dad who hadn't come back from his deployment. His flight suit was displayed in a glass case on the bottom floor of the base education building, surrounded by original nose art from World War II planes, photographs of Vietnam-era generals, and old drawings of the base from the 1940s. Bo always walked quickly by that case when he entered the building, on his way to the library, which was in the back of the ground floor. But he knew that it was a light tan flight suit, the color of a Middle Eastern desert, so that meant the death had been recent, not Vietnam or one of the world wars.

He asked Miss Loupe one more question about cracks on Friday afternoon, moving up to her desk while Trey was still gathering his things.

"How do you know if a crack is good or bad?"

Miss Loupe leaned toward him. "You don't always know. But the first step is finding them."

Bo tried one more time.

"Does your dad still think you made a mistake about the Academy?" he asked.

Miss Loupe was surprised. She looked unsure how to respond.

"He must," she finally answered. "He hasn't spoken to me since."

That weekend, Bo's dad offered him a ride out to the flight line, to meet some jets coming back from a deployment.

He liked riding in his dad's official car, a blue sedan with a white top (so everyone could see the command car coming) and an ever-squawking radio (so his dad could stay on top of flight operations) and a battered thermos of strong coffee (which his dad took everywhere) on the floor of the front seat. The thermos rolled and bumped against Bo's feet as they turned onto the road to the flight line.

When they reached the red lines on the concrete that marked the secured area, his dad stopped and the two of them got out to inspect the car's tires. Anything, even a tiny rock, that stuck in the treads could get dropped on a runway and sucked down a jet engine.

"Why are there cracks in tires, anyway?" asked Bo. "Why don't they make them smooth?"

"You wouldn't be able to keep the car on the road, for one thing," his dad said. "The treads help create friction between the tire and the road."

Bo flicked a chunk of gravel out of one deep groove. He'd just saved the Air Force millions of dollars in damage! Millions! They should pay him to do this.

They climbed back in the car.

"What about the planes? Do they look for cracks in them?"

"All the time, in the engine shop. One undetected crack can mean a lost jet and two dead crewmen."

"What happens if you make a mistake while flying?"

"We train *not* to make mistakes," said his dad.

"But if you do?"

"We use the ejection seat," said his dad. "We train how to use that correctly too."

"What if *that* has a crack in it?" said Bo.

"Better hope you've been living right," said his dad. "But that's not going to happen." He was driving slowly down the side of the runway. "Are you worried about something?"

Bo blinked. Was he?

"I'm proud of how you've managed to keep your nose clean at school so far."

"Well," said Bo. "It's actually . . . better. Miss Loupe is kind of crazy and she lets us get on her couch and play games and —"

His dad looked sideways at him. "What happened to math and reading and all that?"

"Oh, that stuff's still there."

"Hmmm," said his dad. "Well, in any case, I don't think Gari will want to hear about mistakes and cracks when she gets here. Plenty of cracks in her life already, if you know what I mean."

Not really. When Gari got here, if she hung out with the pack of girls in his class and left him alone, she'd be fine.

"Besides that, I don't believe in thinking too much about mistakes. If you do, then that's the only thing in your head. When I fly, I think about what I want to do right, not what I'm trying *not* to do wrong. Same thing when I play golf. I think about where I want the ball to go, not about the sand trap."

He slowed the car and looked at Bo.

"So, here's what you can be thinking about: If you can keep doing the right thing at school, I've arranged for you to meet the Flying Farmer at the air show."

Bo was speechless. He had watched the Flying Farmer with his dad every year at a base air show since he was a little kid. He remembered sitting on his dad's shoulders and nearly ripping every hair from his dad's head when the "hick from the sticks" had "accidentally" swooped off the ground in a supercharged stunt plane. They had both turned around and around, trying to follow the "runaway" plane as it sped in crazy loops over their heads.

"LAND, MR. FARMER! LAND!" he had yelled with the crowd and laughed until he got the hiccups as the "farmer" finally bumped the plane down on the runway and staggered out to faint into the air show marshal's arms. There was nothing better than the Flying Farmer.

"Deal?" said his dad.

"Yes," said Bo.

"Of course, Gari can meet him too. I want her to feel every bit a part of our family."

Bo hoped Gari hated planes. He hoped she would sit in the VIP tent and stuff herself with barbecue and be too comatose to meet anyone. Or maybe she would decide to skip the air show altogether and stay home.

They were approaching the section of the flight line where the jets would park. Families crowded the edge of the runway, waiting for the jets' arrival. Little kids were running around in circles, chasing one another with American flags. Moms who normally lived in sweatsuits had donned short skirts or sleek jeans. Everyone's hair was shiny.

Bo had seconds before his dad got out of the car and became "sir" to everyone within fifty feet.

"Dad, would you not speak to me if I decided not to go to the Air Force Academy?"

"Of course not, Bo." His dad cleared his throat with a flourish. "Now, if you went to the University of Florida . . ."

Bo recoiled in mock horror. The Florida Gators were the legendary enemies of his dad's alma mater, the Volunteers of the University of Tennessee.

"Go VOLS!" he yelled loudly enough to make his dad laugh.

His dad tossed him a pair of earplugs.

The maintainers preparing for the jets' arrival snapped to attention as Colonel Whaley stepped onto the flight line. If the crew had been recovering the commander's jet, they would've kept their overshirts carefully buttoned. But today, they had stripped to the black T-shirts underneath, which Bo thought made them look ultra-cool, like Trey's drawings of superheroes.

Bo recognized Trey's dad as he saluted Colonel Whaley. It felt weird, like he was saluting Bo too. He waved to show Sergeant Obermeyer that he was the same old Bo who came over to hang out with Trey.

Colonel Whaley walked over to let the families know that the jets were due in on time. Bo leaned against the command car and waited. He slipped on his dad's old sunglasses, which were bent from where Bo had sat on them in the car. He pushed the squishy yellow earplugs into his pocket and discovered the beginnings of a tiny hole in the seam of the lining. He counted cracks in the concrete barriers that separated the runway road from the planes' parking spots.

Miss Loupe was right. There were cracks everywhere. And lots of light. He hadn't been to see Mrs. Heard once this year. He was sure Miss Loupe not only tolerated him but *liked* him. He was going to get to meet the Flying Farmer with his dad. Maybe he *wasn't* the same old Bo if you looked closely enough.

The crowd began to press toward the barriers, and Bo heard the roar of jets approaching. He rolled the earplugs into skinny tubes and put them in his ears, where they expanded to muffle the engine noise. He straightened his dad's sunglasses, which skidded down his nose every time he turned his head. Squinting through the green lenses at the sky, he watched a jet drop into the landing pattern. Eyeing the jet carefully, he took a deliberate breath and held it.

I'm underwater. I'm in a room with poison gas. I'm in outer space, looking down at the world.

The plane descended steeply in one long, controlled turn, losing altitude gracefully until it swooped, wings thrown back, above the white line that marked the center of the main runway. Bo's lungs began to demand air, but he narrowed his eyes and focused on the jet's tires.

I'm punching out of a plane. I'm floating down to earth. I'm landing in a desert with no one around for miles and miles. I'm behind enemy lines and they might hear me breathe. . . .

Four . . . three . . . two . . . one . . . PWOOSH! Bo timed his exhale to the two white puffs of dust that marked the instant the jet's tires met the runway and spun upon contact with the ground.

His dad had told him once that the paint alone on an F-15E weighed 500 pounds. Why didn't the whole plane crack the earth when it touched down?

There was a whoop of earplug-dampened noise before the plane slowed to a safe speed and turned toward its parking space, followed seconds later by another plane, and then another. Pilot after pilot was returning home.

A few days later at school, Bo added a small orange-and-white rubber football to Marc's box and inspected the tape on Miss Loupe's floor. It was a solid rectangle. If cracks were important, didn't the Taped Space need some?

When everyone left for lunch, he stayed behind. He tore away two small sections of the tape, about three feet apart from each other. He wadded up the sticky pieces, put them in his pocket, and waited to see what happened next.

10
NOT READY

Gari was sitting high on her mom's bed, on her soft white quilt stitched with interlocking circles, folding star after star and dropping them into a gallon-sized plastic bag.

Her mom was on the floor, struggling to zip up her mobility bag, which was bulging with everything she would need for a year. She finally removed a paperback book, now with a bent cover, and put it on the pile of things that wouldn't fit. She pushed the disposable camera she'd bought down against a line of rolled-up sand-colored T-shirts.

"Hold that end, please. I'm not taking anything else out!"

Gari slid slowly off the bed and knelt down. She pulled the two sides of the oblong camo bag together so her mom could stand over it and yank the zipper closed. The bag finally swallowed her uniforms, her extra pair of glasses, her rubber gas mask, and even her favorite lip balm that she refused to leave behind.

"What about you?" she said to Gari. "Are you all done with your suitcase? Did you remember your retainer? The camera? I want lots of pictures of you in North Carolina!"

"Please, Mom, tell them you aren't ready," Gari said, still kneeling. She looked up. "Tell them I need you. Tell them to make another plan."

Her mom had beads of sweat around the edges of her forehead from struggling with the heavy bag. "I *am* ready. So are you. We have a perfectly good plan. All you have to do is get on the plane tomorrow. Then I'll report to my unit." She held the two cloth handles of the bag together and wrapped them with another rectangle of fabric.

But what about Improvised Explosive Devices? What about short-range missile attacks? What about everything else she had found out by searching for "Iraq" and "war" on the Internet?

Gari stood up and then plopped herself down on top of the bag. "What if I don't? You can't leave if I'm still here, can you?" She stared at her mom's feet, which were encased in the slightly shiny army socks that her mom said fought off foot infections. Her mom had been trying to break in her new light brown desert boots by wearing them a little each day, but she took them off in the house. The boots sat near the bed, their tops flopping over, completing the one uniform her mom had laid out to wear when she left. Gari wished she dared to Super Glue those stupid boots to the carpet.

Her mom reached out and curved her hand over Gari's folded arms.

"Pick your battles, baby. . . ."

Gari shifted her shoulders, but she didn't look up or uncross her arms. She could feel the edge of the camera poking her in the clenched muscle of her left leg. She thought of stars, thousands and thousands of them piling up in their house, making it so full that her mom couldn't leave.

Her mom finished softly, ". . . Or you'll lose them all."

Gari got up and threw herself back on the bed, facedown. Her bag of stars bounced, and some of them flew out, strewing over the quilt. She lay there, focusing on the swirl of stitches that were blurring in front of her eyes.

I KNOW, Mom. I AM picking this one.

11
EVERYONE YOU KNOW

The next morning, as she was about to begin her science lesson — "Ecosystems: Closed or Open?" — Miss Loupe noticed the two gaps in the Taped Space.

She scanned her classroom. Bo looked straight ahead.

"Hmm. Is that a crack?" she said. "Or a door? Hard to tell."

Miss Loupe posted herself, in her cardinal-red shirt, between the class and the rectangle, like a human stop sign.

"But door or no door, our Taped Space is off-limits today," she declared. "No entry. No admittance. No exceptions."

"You're kidding," Bo muttered. He hadn't meant to mess up things that badly. Not today, at least. The circle on his mom's calendar said Gari would be arriving late tonight. His parents had stacked extra stuff from his dad's office along the walls of his bedroom until they could figure out where to put it. They had bought white towels with tiny flowers on them for the bathroom. They had given Indy a bath and made Bo scan the backyard several times for any overlooked poop. He had already gotten in trouble over his attitude about that.

"Why?" Allison demanded.

Miss Loupe smiled. "Why, indeed?" she said. "Why are some

74

systems closed and some are open? What are the boundaries that define an ecosystem or a community?"

She approached the edge of the taped line. Her toes wiggled up and down as if she were itching to jump.

"It's your job," she instructed the class, "to stop me from going in."

She rocked on her heels and swung back her arms.

"But ma'am, you're the teacher," Melissa protested. "That's not fair."

Miss Loupe was swinging her arms forward. . . .

"Don't!" Bo yelled. "It's covered with dog poop!"

"Ohhh," Miss Loupe said as she arrested her jump and wrinkled her nose. "Is it?" She peered into the depths of the Taped Space. "You think dog poop is dangerous?"

"And sharks," added Bo.

"Ah. I guess I'll have to put on my shark-proof diving suit, then." She zipped an imaginary one over her clothes.

"Land mines," Trey called out. "Lots of them!"

"Thank you, Trey. I'll take my explosives detector." She hoisted an imaginary backpack over her shoulder.

"It's sacred ground!" Martina yelled. "No one is allowed to set foot in there!"

"Guess I'd better not use my feet, then," Miss Loupe said. She sat down beside the Taped Space and prepared to roll over the line.

The protests flew from the class like sparks from a sputtering fuse.

"It's electrified!"

"You'll be put in jail!"

"It's against school rules! Page fifteen of the Handbook!"

"Nachos will miss you if you never come back!"

In the middle of the game, Mrs. Heard stuck her head in the doorway.

"Miss Loupe? I heard noise and I . . ."

Miss Loupe scrambled up off the floor. She tucked in her shirt.

"Come in," she said. "We were just discussing boundaries and changes to ecosystems."

Mrs. Heard looked puzzled. She tilted her head toward the Ugly, Ugly Couch.

"I'm sorry, but that needs to be gone before the School Commission comes." As she approached it, she sneezed three times. "There's not a cat in here, is there?" She pulled a tissue from her suit pocket and pressed it to her nose. "And I need your report for the Commission as soon as possible."

After Mrs. Heard left, Room 208 protested.

"She can't take away the couch! We need it!"

"What's wrong with having a couch in here?"

Bo said, "Mrs. Heard is a crazy, old —"

Miss Loupe jumped into the Taped Space with both feet. The class was instantly silenced.

"'Be kind,'" she said, "'for everyone you know is fighting a great battle.'"

"Who said that?" Allison asked. "Some famous general?"

"Philo of Alexandria, an ancient Greek philosopher," Miss Loupe said.

"What battle?" said Trey, looking up from the drawing he had begun of Mrs. Heard dueling with a gigantic fanged cat.

"That's the thing," Miss Loupe said. "Everyone's fighting a different one." She looked over at the picture on her desk. "Of course, Marc would say he's in a battle. But so would Miss Candy."

"Miss Candy?" Zac said. "How?"

"Well, why do you think she's building a castle in her library when nobody's asked her to?" Miss Loupe said. "You don't build a castle if you're not fighting something."

"But Mrs. Heard is in charge of everything," Allison objected. "What's she fighting?"

"Something practically invisible," Miss Loupe said. "An idea. A long-established idea about how much money an old school next to an Air Force base should get."

"What about you, ma'am?" Melissa said. "Are you in a battle?"

"Of course, Melissa, of course."

But Miss Loupe didn't say what it was. Instead, she perched on the edge of the Ugly, Ugly Couch and patted its cushions gently.

"Don't worry about the couch. I'll ask Miss Candy if we can store it behind the castle wall she's building. After the School Commission visits, I'll petition Mrs. Heard to move it back into our classroom. I think she'll let us because we'll have given her lots of ammunition to use in her funding battle, won't we?"

She hoisted the hefty packet of paper for the report.

"Everybody's going to help me finish this by Friday, right? Everybody knows where the cracks are around here."

They did.

Then, because it was his last day and his mom was picking him up early, Miss Loupe invited Dillon up to sit on the Ugly, Ugly Couch and be interviewed. Allison volunteered to ask the questions.

"So, Dillon, before you go, would you like to tell us who your favorite person in Miss Loupe's class is?" she said, tilting an imaginary microphone close to his mouth. She smoothed her white skirt and looked sideways at him from her carefully arranged position on the edge of one dingy cushion.

"No," he said. "I wouldn't."

Allison giggled. "Well, how about your favorite person on this couch?"

Dillon looked frantically to Miss Loupe for help. She turned to the rest of the class.

"Anybody have an interesting question for Dillon? About where he's going? Or what he's enjoyed here at Young Oaks?"

Aimee raised her hand. "How about if you do Miss/Won't Miss? That's fun."

"Oh, totally cool, Aimee," said Allison, nodding her approval. "I *so* invented that game. First one, Dillon: the Young Oaks Bear. Miss or won't miss?"

"Miss," said Dillon. "He's ugly, but at least he's huge and scary-looking. My last school had a caterpillar for a mascot!"

"The lunchroom," Bo called out.

"Miss," Dillon said immediately. "They're probably going to serve sauerkraut at my new school." He made a gagging noise deep in his throat. "But maybe the hot dogs there won't bounce if you drop them."

"Our hot dogs *bounce*?" said Allison. She started to ask a follow-up question, but Melissa interrupted.

"Homework," Melissa said.

"Won't miss," Dillon said. "Duh."

"Jet noise!" Trey yelled.

"Won't miss. 'Cause it'll still be there," Dillon answered. "We're living on base again."

"Your desk," Kylie said.

Dillon wondered if the next person who sat in it would make the crack he had deepened even larger. "Won't miss."

"The Ugly, Ugly Couch," Rick offered.

"Miss," Dillon said, grabbing a couch pillow and laying his cheek against it with feigned passion. Everybody laughed, and Dillon looked surprised. He added, "Yeah. I'd like to see what you guys do with this thing for the rest of the year."

Miss Loupe stepped forward. "Would you and Allison stand up, please?" she said.

When they had moved out of the way, she stood behind the Ugly, Ugly Couch and pushed down hard on its back until the front two legs left the floor.

"Look under there," she said.

The underside of the couch was covered with people's names. The class crowded forward to see. Miss Loupe explained that some of them were the cast members of the two plays the couch had been in after it left the movies. She also showed them where

Marc had signed it, and all his Army friends, the day they watched the Super Bowl together before deploying. Nachos had left a salsa-stained paw print. One name, Eric Browne, had a little heart beside it. Miss Loupe admitted he was an old boyfriend.

Miss Loupe handed Dillon a permanent marker. "You'll be the first one from Young Oaks. Anywhere you like."

After Dillon had signed, and his mom had picked him up, Miss Loupe once again entered the Taped Space and addressed the class. "Before we get back to our science lesson, I have an announcement." She flushed pink to her ears. "I . . . well, I'm a finalist for an arts grant to teach improvisational theater! I just found out yesterday!"

She looked so pleased that half the class broke into applause, even though they weren't quite sure what this meant for Room 208.

"What's improvisational theater?" asked Melissa.

"It's what we've been doing every afternoon," said Miss Loupe. She grinned. "You know, when I put my weird slippers on. Some people call it 'improv' for short. You could say it was just games, scenes, and making up things as you go along. That would be true."

Miss Loupe stepped closer to her class. "But you could also say that it's about counting on one another. Counting on one another to say 'Yes, and . . .' Counting on one another to see cracks as doors. Counting on one another to turn battles into stories."

"I don't get it," said Allison.

"That's okay," said Miss Loupe. "I don't know everything yet either." She turned and wrote another saying on the chalkboard:

One does not discover new lands
without consenting to lose sight of the shore. . . .
— André Gide

"What does 'consent' mean?" asked Aimee.

"To say yes," said Miss Loupe. "Dillon, for example, is definitely consenting to discover new lands." She spread out her arms as wide as on the first day of class. "When we do improv, so can we."

Her voice and energy flooded the room. Bo wondered how he had ever thought she was tiny.

Miss Loupe's words tumbled out faster. "In order to receive the money, I have to prove that the project I'm proposing will be . . ." She grabbed a piece of paper off her desk and read from it. "'. . . an innovative approach to youth arts education, specific to the needs of an underserved environment, and a significant contribution to the community as a whole.'" She put the paper down and took a deep breath. "What that means is: I want to start a youth improv troupe at Young Oaks and run a free theater camp here in Reform. And I need your help."

Bo's stomach flipped in a loop the loop. Cool. Theater camp. He had a flash of himself getting a starring role. Something good that people would remember.

"I'll tell you a secret," Miss Loupe continued. "When I was here in Reform in the sixth grade, I hated being here. I thought there was nothing to do. I didn't know I would find theater. I didn't know I would become a teacher. I was miserable." She looked around her class. "I want those of you who will love theater all your life to find out sooner than I did. And I want this school to succeed.

"So I'll be leading theater activities here in Room 208. I want all of you to be involved. And if that goes well, and the grant money is approved, I hope you all will discover new lands with me at theater camp next summer."

She patted the couch. "I'd like to call our improv troupe the Ugly Couch Players. If you consent, of course." She smiled and looked invitingly at the class.

But Bo had stopped listening.

Next summer?

Next summer?

His dad was getting an assignment at the end of the school year. Bo was going to be *gone* next summer.

He felt himself fall into a steep, engineless dive.

His name might get written under the couch when he left, like Dillon. But no matter what Miss Loupe said, no matter what he did this year, it would all disappear. He would soon be on the outside, of Reform, of Young Oaks, of everything. He'd always known it; it was all he'd ever known, moving so much. But he saw it clearly for the first time, like a giant crack that had been forming all along: The Taped Space could be peeled right up, and so could he.

12
LAST DAY IN SEATTLE

At the airport, Gari's mom pressed an ancient-looking, dark green plastic army figure into Gari's hand.

"I want you to have this," she said.

Gari nodded. She didn't trust any of the words that were rising up in her throat. She felt like if she said any of them, she would start throwing up and not be able to stop.

"My commander gave this to me the day I left the Army for the civilian world," her mom said. "She told me I didn't have to put in my papers, and that I could always come back."

She wrapped Gari's fingers around the army figure and squeezed her hand. "At the time, I couldn't give everything to the Army and to a baby too, so I chose you. Now, maybe I can give something that I couldn't give then. Do you understand?"

Gari didn't dare look at the battered figure. She didn't want to cry in front of all these people. She shoved it into her pocket.

"All the time," her mom said.

Gari couldn't say anything, not even the response her mom was waiting for.

So she allowed her mom to hug her so hard that her chest hurt. She allowed the attendant at the airline desk to use her camera to take a picture of her and her mom, arms around each other as if nothing were happening. She allowed her feet to walk her body onto the airplane and the plane to lift her off the ground.

I know I have to leave. I know you have to go too. But I'm coming back. So are you. Mom, we have to have a Plan B.

PLAN
B

13

IF ALARM SIGNAL SOUNDS

Bo tried to explain to Gari what a waste of time Miss Loupe's class was.

"There's this stupid Taped Space, and she'll try to get you all interested in it," he began, but Gari groaned.

"It's four o'clock in the morning," she said, leaning her head against the car window. "In Seattle, it's four o'clock in the morning."

She didn't even bother looking out the window as they drove slowly out of base housing toward the main gate. All the houses looked exactly alike anyway. Gari closed her eyes and stroked Indy's fur. Bo's dog was the only part of North Carolina that she liked. The dog, which was snuggled on her lap in the front seat, let out a whimper of support and licked her face.

Normally, her aunt had told her, she and Bo would be walking to school, along with most of the kids who lived on the base.

"But I'll drive you today so we can take care of your paperwork."

Ugh. Walking. That probably meant getting up even earlier. Yesterday, Aunt Donna and Uncle Phil had let her stay home since her flight had gotten in late the night before, and she hadn't adjusted to East Coast time. She'd wanted to stay home this morning too, because who starts school on a Friday? But Aunt Donna had sent Indy into Gari's bedroom. The dog had jumped up onto her bed and licked her neck until she had had to struggle out from under the covers. She had splashed some water on her face and then sat in the kitchen staring at a glass of orange juice instead of drinking it. Beside the glass was the house key Uncle Phil had given her. The key was attached to a bright red nylon strip of stiff cloth that had bold white letters on it: REMOVE BEFORE FLIGHT.

"Bo has one," he'd said. "We all do. It makes the key hard to lose." He had smiled, but all Gari could think was how much his voice sounded like her mom's. And her mom wasn't there.

In the car, Gari opened one eye and glanced at herself in the little mirror on the sunshade. Brown curls sticking out every which way, red cat-eye glasses, and her old but comfy jeans with a plain green T-shirt. She still had crease marks on her cheeks from the pillow.

Bo was going on about how the Taped Space (whatever that was) was only good for DYING in and then if she ever wondered if a crack would open up and swallow her, and she squeezed her one eye shut again and put her head deep into Indy's fur.

"Bo," his mom said, "what on earth are you talking about? You're supposed to be welcoming Gari, not scaring her to death." She said to Gari, "Don't worry. I've called the counselor and they're expecting us this morning. Everything will be fine."

"Can you tell the counselor I want to take Japanese?" Gari asked, lifting her mouth away from Indy's sleek coat. "Everybody at Seattle Junior Academy is taking that this year."

"Yeah, and tell him I want to drop out," Bo said.

Bo's mom gave him a piercing look in the rearview mirror as she turned on her blinker and approached the school.

Indy shifted in Gari's lap, her hind paws digging into Gari's jeans as she pressed her front paws against the window. Despite herself, Gari opened her eyes and looked at Young Oaks.

That old hodgepodge of brick buildings? There were hardly any windows! There was nothing "young" about it.

They parked in a spot between an oversized van with a bumper sticker that read JET NOISE: THE SOUND OF FREEDOM and a pink VW Bug with a yellow ribbon tied to its antenna. There were larger, and more faded, yellow ribbons tied around the huge twin oak trees at the school's entrance.

Indy tried to get out of the car when Gari did, but Mrs. Whaley pulled her back in.

"You wait here, good dog." She stuffed a jump rope and a book called *Great Games!* into the glove compartment before rolling the window down a crack and locking the door. "Don't eat anything."

Gari wished she could stay in the car too. Or the glove compartment. It didn't matter, as long as she could sleep.

As they walked into the school, Bo narrated in a television announcer's voice, "On your left, the oldest flagpole in America! To your right, the Young Oaks mascot, the rarely seen Rusted Bear. As we enter the building —"

89

"Bo, stop it," his mom warned. "Go to class. Gari will be there in a little bit."

But she wasn't. The counselor needed the original, not faxed, document giving Colonel and Mrs. Whaley legal guardianship of Gari. Her school in Seattle hadn't sent any records, so how could she be placed in the right classroom, especially after the school year had already begun? And where were Gari's proof of vaccination and her school physical?

By the time Mrs. Whaley had rushed home to retrieve Gari's forgotten medical records (and put Indy in the backyard), promised to have the original guardianship document sent directly to the school, and gotten confirmation from Principal Heard that Gari was supposed to be (as promised) in the same class as her cousin, it was mid-morning. Mrs. Whaley was going to be late to her job teaching P.E. at another school.

"Miss Loupe's room is down that hallway there," she told Gari. "Bo can show you around once you see him."

Great. Now she would enter the classroom in the middle of a lesson, and everyone would turn and stare at her. And then they would expect her to say something about who she was, and where she was from, and why she was there, and . . . Gari's throat went dry just thinking about it. Why couldn't she be at SeaJA, where she and Tandi had planned to march in together and nobody would expect her to stand up in front of anyone?

But when Gari finally arrived in Room 208, it was empty. Bo hadn't told anyone to wait for her. There was an odd rectangle of masking tape on the floor at the front of the classroom — what had Bo been saying about the tape? That someone *died* in it?

What was a couch doing in a classroom? It looked like a refu-
gee from a furniture clearance sale, and it smelled like . . .
pretzels? Bagel chips? What was that odor?

Gari dropped her book bag on the floor and flopped onto
the ugly couch. The cushions were deep and soft. She curled her
body into a ball and tucked her head against one of the fringed
throw pillows.

If someone comes, I'll . . . I'll . . .

She was awakened by squeals. A boy was poking her in
the head.

"I'm Tony," he was saying. "Who are you?"

"Is she my Reading Buddy? I don't want *her!*" some other
kid said.

Gari stared up at them from her horizontal viewpoint, adjust-
ing her glasses from where they had slipped off her face. These
kids were much younger than she was, maybe six . . . maybe
seven years old?

"What grade am I in?" she said. She struggled to sit up from
the squishy cushions.

A strange-looking teacher was clapping his freckled hands.

"Mr. Nix's class, Mr. Nix's class! Pay attention! There has
been a miscommunication. Our Reading Buddies are not here.
We shall go tell Miss Candy and see if she —"

His words were cut off by the wailing sound of an alarm.
Gari covered her ears.

OO-GAH! OO-GAH! OO-GAH!

"Fire drill, class, fire drill," Mr. Nix announced. "Make two
parallel lines."

The students formed one solid clump at the door.

Mr. Nix shook his head in dismay and tried to divide them into two nonintersecting lines.

"The Forest of Foggy Thinking," Mr. Nix was muttering, "how quickly it sprouts!"

The fire alarm kept blaring. *OO-GAH! OO-GAH! OO-GAH!*

Finally, Mr. Nix commanded: "First graders! Move out!" and they streamed through the door.

"You too, young lady," he said to Gari, who was still on the couch. "No one stays in the building during a fire drill. Page twenty-one!"

Page twenty-one? Of what? Is he using a code so the first graders don't panic?

She found herself standing outside, in a bare spot next to a dilapidated jungle gym, surrounded by giddy first graders. They hopped up and down while Mr. Nix tried to show them the correct fire drill formation by pointing out parallel limbs on a nearby pine tree.

"THAT is how straight your lines should be!"

"I fell out of a tree," said a boy. "I have a scab."

"A bird!" said a bouncing girl. "I see a bird! I'd like to BE a bird!"

"We're not discussing birds," said Mr. Nix. "Or falling out of trees. I'm simply pointing out that —"

"Mr. Nix, do you have any scabs?" said the boy who had poked Gari in the head.

"No, I —"

"Or tattoos? My sister says her teacher has a bird tattooed on her —"

Two jets roared overhead, drowning out all sound. A few of the kids whooped as they flew over. Gari winced.

Why did they let them fly over the school? They were so loud!

The jets left two tails of exhaust in the sky.

"Do you see that?" Mr. Nix said. "Parallel lines!"

When they were allowed back in the building, Mr. Nix instructed Gari to go to the office and report that she had been found without a hall pass in an empty classroom.

"On page thirty-two," Mr. Nix said, "it clearly states: 'Every student should remain with his or her class unless given written permission to be elsewhere.'"

Oh, yes. Clearly. Now if someone would tell me which book . . .

But she didn't want to risk a lecture on Foggy Forests, so she silently headed for the office, not to turn herself in, but to put into place another plan: calling Aunt Donna's cell phone and begging to go home. It was a decent plan, but not well executed. She took a left turn at the third water fountain instead of a right and ended up in the cafeteria.

A woman in a neat white polo shirt was peering at a crack in the side of the cash register. Underneath her hairnet were rows of wavy gray curls. She was holding a bottle of gold nail polish.

"Can't fix it," she was saying to no one in particular. "Might as well make it look pretty." She dabbed the gold polish delicately into the fissure.

When she noticed Gari, she tilted her head. Her tiny cross earrings bobbled. "Oh, I thought Melissa was helping today."

Gari had no idea who Melissa was, but the lady was now gesturing toward a stack of printed lunch menus.

"Would you be a dear and take those around to the classrooms, please?"

Gari would've protested this request, but there was a leftover cinnamon roll from breakfast on top of the menus, and she hadn't eaten anything since last night. Her stomach was starting to hurt. *It's breakfast time in Seattle anyway,* she thought.

Plus, she'd remembered one thing: She didn't have her aunt's cell phone number. On to the next plan: Deliver the menus and see if she could stumble upon Bo and the rest of her class. They had to be somewhere in the school . . . and Bo would know his mom's number. . . .

Gari delivered the paper-clipped stacks of menus to each classroom, finding her way around the school by fits and starts. The old building looked like it had been added on to several times without any thought to straight, orderly hallways. The ceilings dipped in the middle, and the cinder block walls were rubbed smooth at the corners where thousands of fingers had brushed them.

"Have you seen Miss Loupe's class?" she asked each teacher as she handed them the menus. "They weren't in Room 208."

Nobody seemed to have any idea where they might be. Several of the teachers were too busy to even hear her question, and most of them thought she was there to pick up a document for the principal. Teacher after teacher kept handing her thick, stapled packets.

The bathroom in the kindergarten hall STINKS! one document said on the first page. *It smells so bad we had to block it off and not use it at all. Then I have to walk my class EVEN FARTHER down the hall!*

The railing on my chalkboard has been broken for FIVE years, another one read. *And I need more small desks!*

CRACKS! was written on one in large black letters. *I'm not counting them all, but come and see my ceiling for yourself!*

One frazzled kindergarten teacher apologized to Gari for not having the document ready. "That alarm makes me crazy. Once it starts going off, it won't stop. Some kid figured that out last year, and —" She broke off and asked Gari, please, would she roll this audiovisual cart back to the library, and then come back in about an hour?

The library! The first graders had said something about "Reading Buddies." Maybe the librarian knew where Miss Loupe's class was. Gari stacked the growing pile of papers on the middle shelf of the cart and wheeled it down the hall in search of the library. She rolled past the bathroom that *STINKS!* She could smell it even when the door was shut. She rolled faster.

When she found the library, the place was a lot noisier than she had expected. There was a large sign at the entrance that read CASTLE UNDER CONSTRUCTION: PLEASE EXCUSE OUR MESS. A power saw buzzed at the rear of the room over the sound of steady hammering.

"You must be a new student," said a woman in a smock covered with paint splotches. "I'm the librarian, Miss Candy. And yes, I *do* believe in candy."

She held out a dish of butterscotch drops in one hand while pulling the checkout card for the cart with the other. Gari shook her head. The cinnamon roll in her stomach had made it feel worse, not better.

Miss Candy's eyes flicked from the teacher's name on the card to Gari's face. "But you're not in kindergarten! Whose room are you in?"

"Miss Loupe's," Gari said. "But —"

"Oh, they were here with Mr. Nix's class!" Miss Candy pushed the cart into the storage room. "We had to start late, because Mr. Nix got mixed up, but once they got here, Miss Loupe's class did a marvelous job! Miss Loupe taught everyone how to turn a book into a script, and then they all performed *Pinkerton, Behave!* I don't think I've laughed so hard since school started!"

"But where are they now? Are they back in Room 208?" Gari looked around the storage room. It was piled with videos and books with sticky notes attached to them. There was a giant reference book about castles and several rolled-up posters.

"No, they were going to lunch. But some of them will be back here later, because they have to put the couch behind the castle wall."

"Oh," Gari said. She wondered how many couches were in this school. And why was one going behind a wall?

Miss Candy looked hard at Gari's face. "I heard Bo's cousin

was coming to stay with him. Is that you? Your mom's deployed —"

OO-GAH! OO-GAH! OO-GAH!

"*Frog and Toad!*" Miss Candy said. "Not again!" She motioned Gari out of the storage room and called to the two young men who were working at the back of the library. "Airman Peters, Airman Kresge! I'm sorry, I know you've only got a few hours to volunteer, but we have to quit and go outside."

She hurriedly locked the storage room door, picked up her purse from behind the checkout desk, and stuffed a handful of butterscotch drops into the pocket of her smock.

"Want me to see if I can fix it?" said one of the men. He had on a black T-shirt and camo pants.

"Dude, don't do it. You know these kids love getting out of class," the other airman said.

The alarm suddenly stopped, and Gari was surprised when Miss Candy and the two airmen kept going toward the exit door at the back of the library.

"It's taking a breath," said Miss Candy. "Wait and see."

"Miss Candy," Gari said, looking hurriedly at the books as she passed by them, "does the library have anything about Iraq?"

They emerged from the back of the school into the hot, sticky air.

"We do have some general books on the Middle East, with sections about Iraq. Maybe a bit on Islamic art in a reference book too. We don't have much."

"Art? Do you have a lot of —"

A woman in a brown suit was bearing down on them. She was large and solid, like Gari's mom's lumbering Subaru.

"Principal Heard," Miss Candy greeted her.

Gari's stomach jumped and then swirled around and around.

"There you are," said Mrs. Heard. "Miss Loupe sent word that a lamb was on the lam. But I knew I could corral you." She took Gari by the arm and led her to a group of students flowing out of the double doors.

"Miss Loupe," she called. "I've found her!"

That tiny person is my teacher? thought Gari as they approached. *Look at her hair!*

"Do you prefer to be called Gari or Garrison?" Miss Loupe was saying. "Bo didn't tell us."

Gari looked down the line for Bo. There he was, or at least the back of his head. He was deliberately looking away from her.

Gari swallowed and started to answer.

OO-GAH! OO-GAH! OO-GAH! The alarm kicked off again.

Principal Heard said to Miss Loupe, "Go ahead and take your class back inside. I'm calling off this fire drill because our alarm is obviously malfunctioning." She looked hard at Bo, who was intent upon flattening the dandelions around him with the heel of his shoe.

The class began filing back into the building, and Gari slipped into line beside Bo. There wasn't much choice, since she didn't know anyone else.

"I need your mom's cell number," she said. "Now."

Bo kept walking. He was focused on the back of the girl in front of them, a girl whose long hair swung from side to side as she picked her way through the grass, avoiding dirt patches. She was covering her ears with cupped hands.

OO-GAH! OO-GAH! OO-GAH!

Gari pushed her glasses hard against her nose. Her stomach felt as if the alarm were pulsing inside it.

"Bo, I want to go home!"

"Me too," he said.

"But you'll miss improv!" said a girl behind them.

Bo shrugged and didn't answer her.

"What's improv?" said Gari. "Can't I miss that?"

"No. You have to say 'yes, and —'" He kicked at a patch of dandelion weeds, sending fluff into the air. "Even if you don't want to."

Gari stopped dead outside the double metal doors. "Okay, then: Yes, and — I feel terrible and I want to go home."

OO-GAH! OO — The alarm stopped once more. The girl in front of them uncovered her ears.

"Fine," said Bo. "Try jumping out a window. That works."

Gari shoved her hand into her pocket. Her fingers tightened around the little green army figure she had stowed away, and she did what her mom always did when she was serious about a request. She used Bo's full name.

"Just give me the number, Bogart!"

"Bogart?" said the girl. She paused at the door and turned around. "BOGART?" she said even louder. She giggled.

"What's your problem?" said Gari. "I'm not talking to you. I'm talking to Bog —"

Bo poked her, hard, in the stomach. "Shut *up!*"

All the pain in Gari's stomach expanded, like a balloon filling with a rush of helium. *OO-GAH! OO-GAH! OO-GAH!* The alarm kicked back in, and Gari threw up, in a continuous wave, on the oh-so-cute navy-blue shoes of the girl who had giggled.

"She barfed on my shoes!" the girl shrieked, as loudly as the alarm. "What's-Her-Name barfed on my new shoes!"

Bo looked up from the cinnamon-colored liquid swirling over Allison's shoes. Miss Loupe was standing inside the door, holding it ajar for the class. She'd seen everything.

That wasn't what I . . .

Maybe she would . . .

Then he noticed that she was looking at something behind him. A large brown-suited arm reached past him.

"Allison, that's enough. Your shoes can be cleaned up," said Mrs. Heard, handing her a fistful of tissues. "Hold these over your mouth," she continued, giving a wad to Gari, "but you'd better get to the nurse." She pinched Bo's shoulder. "*You* can come with me."

14
DECEASED INSECTS

They were supposed to go to Hog Heaven that night. They didn't.

For one thing, Gari said that even though she felt a little better, she couldn't go because she was a vegetarian.

"If I were a hog," she said to Bo, "that's not what I'd call heaven: my guts, chopped on a bun!"

Mrs. Whaley made her a hummus sandwich, which Gari didn't eat either.

But the main reason they didn't go to Hog Heaven was because Bo wasn't finished wiping each windowsill clear of the stiff flies and curled wasps that died in the groove between the screen and window glass during the hot fall weather. He battled the hard specks of gnats spotting the transom with a rag and torrents of cleaning spray. He ran one rag-circled finger around the edges of the screen, soaking dirt and crushed bug parts up for transport to the trash bag he trailed from window to window. Indy kept poking her nose into each frame as he worked.

He couldn't explain to his dad why he'd made Gari throw up. He hadn't planned to. He hadn't meant to.

"It was her *first day*," his dad had said. "Her mom is halfway around the world *serving her country*. She's your cousin, as good as your *sister*."

Bo hadn't said a word. He felt like he did when the sky turned not black but puke green before a storm. That had happened twice this past spring, before a tornado warning had gone off for the entire base. The good things he did — like helping Sanjay when he couldn't think of a line in the Taped Space, or this morning, letting Indy curl up in Gari's lap instead of his on the way to school — all that faded fast. He wished he could be like the Flying Farmer and have all his mistakes come out right in the end. His dad hadn't mentioned the stunt pilot, but Bo knew. Their deal was . . . well . . . out the window.

Meanwhile, Gari tried to drink a little ginger ale at the kitchen counter and paged through the local papers that Aunt Donna had stacked to recycle. Not much exciting in the *Reform Chronicle*. A barbecue cook-off. A wreck with no injuries near the base gate. A two-page guide to football games. No protests against this stupid war . . . of course not, not in a base town. Only a splashy story about a squadron homecoming.

In a small insert, there was more base news and ads for a fall sale at the Base Exchange store. The only interesting thing was the "Security Forces Blotter." Gari read about a shoplifting incident at a base snack bar, "a minor dependent" being banned from housing for vandalism, and a fight at a club, which resulted in a charge of "insubordination." She wondered if the Security Forces reported trouble outside the base too, like at the school. If so, Bo's name should be in there in big letters.

When Bo was done with the de-bugging, he went to the master bedroom, where his dad was working. Colonel Whaley had moved his desk against one wall, squeezed stacks of paper underneath it, and piled books on either side. Bo held up the nearly empty spray bottle and the crusty rag. His dad, phone pressed to one ear, nodded.

Bo threw the rag into the laundry basket on top of the washer and put the bottle away on the shelf above. He wanted to go to Trey's house. He wanted to slam golf balls onto a chunk of concrete and watch them shoot into the air, over and over. But his mom . . . she had WORK for him too.

She held out three ropes with bright blue handles. "Would you and Gari help me try out a jump rope game? I need to practice before I teach my first graders on Monday."

Bo knew what his mom was trying to do. So did Gari. She said no, that her stomach couldn't take any more jumping. She set down her glass of ginger ale and went into her room and shut the door. He could hear her talking on her cell phone, *blah, blah, blah* to her friend back in Seattle. *Blah, blah,* you wouldn't believe how *blah blah.* But he had to take the jump ropes from his mom.

His mom's WORK — even though she called it just talking — was worse than his dad's.

"Jump on one foot," said his mom.

She had backed both cars out of the garage, so they could jump in there and avoid the mosquitoes that came with the darkening sky. One wall was stacked with cardboard boxes, each labeled with its contents. Stuff they had chosen not to unpack here, stuff his mom was saving for her "forever house," stuff from when he was a baby, which his mom couldn't bear to throw away.

"Now the other foot."

He did. Their ropes slapped against the concrete floor. The overhead light made a circle of brightness around them.

"Both feet!

"Now, side to side, knees together like you've got to pee!"

He stepped on the rope and it thudded to a stop.

"You can't say that, Mom. Not to first graders."

"Why not?" She stopped jumping.

"Because some of them *will*."

Her laughter filled the garage. She nearly knocked over his dad's golf clubs and Indy's travel crate when she put out a hand to steady herself.

"Bo. *Really*." She took the jump rope and halfheartedly tried to lasso him with it. He dodged her throw.

"Mom, do you want to move next summer?"

"No, not especially. I like my job. I like the people here. But I like seeing new places too. I vote for Paris!"

"There isn't a base there. We don't speak French."

"I know. But ever since I saw Humphrey Bogart in *Casablanca*, I've wanted to go there. So I could say: 'We'll always have Paris.'"

He'd seen the ancient black-and-white movie his mom was talking about. He didn't like it. His mom always cried when the plane took off, even though there was way too much fog for a plane to take off in real life. He didn't think his dad liked the movie either. But they both sat there with his mom on her birthday this past year and survived it.

"You don't like being called Bogart, do you?" she said. "Miss Loupe said you seemed upset because —"

"I'm fine. Really," he said. "I can deal with it." *As long as you don't TALK about it.*

His mom bunched up her jump rope, folding it back and forth, back and forth. Her motion made shadows on the wall of boxes behind her. Each box had a red stamp-sized moving sticker on it with a number. Some boxes had more than one sticker, each color layered over the next, where a box had been saved and moved more than once.

How did his mom do it? Start over and over, each time they moved? Didn't she mind being ripped up?

He changed the subject. "Where *are* we going next summer, Mom? Doesn't Dad have any idea?"

"Of course. Otherwise, we might have worried more about Gari coming here to live with us."

What? What did that mean? Bo realized that Aunt Paula wouldn't be back until September, so when they moved next summer, Gari would have to move with them. Did she know that? What had his parents talked about after they had said yes?

"Dad might be offered command of a wing in Afghanistan," his mom said. "It would be a remote assignment, for a year."

The dead center of Bo's chest tightened. Afghanistan? That was as dangerous as where Gari's mom was. He thought of the tan flight suit in the glass case at the library.

"But . . ." Bo couldn't think of a way to talk about that case with his mom. "But . . . what about us? Where would we go?"

Mrs. Heard allowed students to place a sticker on the map of the United States in the front hallway of Young Oaks when they moved. Bo had hoped his sticker would be in Hawaii or Florida, where he could go to the beach, or Colorado, where he could learn to ski. Where did you go if the Air Force didn't tell you where you had to go?

"We might stay here."

"In this house?"

"The next commander gets this house. We would find a place to rent off base. I could keep working at my job. Gari wouldn't have to uproot again, and she could stay with us through the summer and early fall until her mom gets back. You could start middle school here. Would you want to do that?"

Bo didn't know. He could be in the Ugly Couch Players, but . . . did he want to stay here if it meant his dad left? Somewhere in those boxes on the wall was a lumpy, one-eyed, stuffed bear wearing a flight suit. He had been three when his dad had gone to the Middle East for the first time, and he hadn't understood any of it, but he had carried that bear until it stunk and the flight suit had torn and he had fed it jelly beans at Easter, which stained its mouth orange.

"Nothing's settled, " said his mom. "Maybe he won't have to go. Maybe we'll get another stateside assignment. We'll have to wait and see."

She straightened her jump rope. "Ready to try it again?"

After they came back inside, damp from jumping in the humid air, Bo sat at the kitchen counter and ate sliced sweet pickles from the jar. His dad came in and stole three.

"You know," said his dad, eating his pickles one at a time, "you don't *always* have to do the first thing that comes into your head. You can set your own course. Write out what you can do to make Gari feel at home, if you have to. But I don't want a repeat of today."

"No, sir," said Bo.

His mom passed through. "I checked on Gari. She's fine. I'm taking a shower," she said. "Don't let Indy track in mud if you let her out." She opened a drawer and handed them each a fork. "We have clean utensils."

After she left, they passed the jar back and forth, fishing out pickles with their fingers.

"I'm giving you a second chance," said his dad. "A mulligan. So think hard about your choices for the next two weeks, okay? The Flying Farmer would really like to meet his biggest fan."

What? Their deal wasn't off? Why?

He started to ask, then stopped. He knew.

Afghanistan.

It must be happening. Why else would his dad have gone soft? It felt weird, like the boundaries of his world had shifted. He was seeing into his dad's head, which had never happened before.

They took two straws and drank the pickle liquid with giant

slurps, in a stomach-churning race to the bottom. They wiped their hands on their shirts and put the forks in the dishwasher as if they had used them.

He could stay. He could stay and be in the Ugly Couch Players. Why did that feel so bad?

15
NOTHING TO SHOW YOU

Gari was lying on her back on the floor next to her suitcase, her feet propped up on the bed, talking into her cell phone. But she wasn't talking to Tandi. She'd forgotten that it was only six o'clock in Seattle, and Tandi would be at track practice.

But once she had the phone in her hand, she didn't want to put it down. Aunt Donna might insist that she jump rope with Bo in the garage. Like she could forget what he'd done to her that easily. Her aunt didn't know what it was like to throw up at school. How the thin white tissues the principal gave you stuck to your lips. How humiliating it was to sit in the office, waiting to be picked up, like you were a kindergartner who had peed her pants.

"You wouldn't believe how old the school is," she said loudly into the phone, picturing Tandi on the other end. "Yeah, like thousands of years old.

"Uh-huh. Get this: On the road from the airport, I counted seven billboards for restaurants with cartoon pigs on them. In clothes. Yeah, overalls. Pink dresses. Little checkered neckerchiefs. If they think pigs are cute, why do they eat them?"

She stared up at the blank ceiling. There was no light fixture, just an expanse of whiteness, from wall to cleanly painted wall.

"Did you make more stars? Did you ask Jaiden to help you? He likes you. You know he does. Don't tell the other girls — then they won't vote for you. Yeah, I'm making more stars too. I'll mail them to you.

"No. No, I haven't heard from her yet. It takes a long time to get there. She said it might be three days. I don't know. She said she'd send pictures. She said she'd call. She said . . ."

She rested her head against the side of the suitcase. Its handle pressed into her cheek. She snapped the phone closed.

She flopped over and fished around for the book that she had stuffed in her suitcase at the last minute. The one her mom had left behind, the one with the bent cover and the picture of a long-haired vampire on the front.

She read the first chapter.

Holy crap! Why did her mom want to read this? Blood and more blood!

She put the book back in the suitcase and took out her camera. There was exactly one picture used up on the roll.

She took the battered army figure from her pocket and set it on top of the suitcase. She framed it through the lens of the camera.

No.

She moved the figure to the white-and-gold dresser. To the back of the closet cleared of everything but a row of tan plastic hangers. To the nightstand with the rectangular alarm clock on it.

She put down the camera and picked up the clock. She dialed it back to Seattle time. She wished she could dial herself back to when her camera had taken the first picture.

I know you want pictures, Mom. But there's nothing to show you. Nothing.

Aunt Donna tapped on the door.

"You need anything, sweetie?"

"No. I'm going to read."

Gari slid herself under the stiff, quilted, red-white-and-blue cover. The sheets smelled new. The pillow was too high under her neck.

She read another chapter of the vampire book. It was awful. But she stayed inside its pages as Taps played outside. Her mom had said she'd love the music; said she might even want to learn to play the song on her trumpet. But the slow, mournful notes made Gari wish for a giant, thrumming rainstorm to drown out every moment of it.

She stayed inside the book all night. It didn't get any better. Gari wondered if the author had planned anything out, or just let someone die and then become un-dead every few pages. Even the books she'd read in third and fourth grade had more of a point, like *Frindle*. She should send her mom that one.

At five in the morning, Gari tore out the last page of the paperback, which was blank. She dug a pen out of her backpack. She wrote:

My plan to get out of here

Did they stop you going out the gate as well as in? She didn't think so, but there were yellow-and-black-striped barriers that could pop out of the ground and puncture a truck's tires. Bo had explained the popping to her in great detail.

Besides, the key to a successful plan was not her leaving, because she could easily be sent back. It was her mom coming home. If her mom came back to the States, then Gari could return to Seattle with her. But what would bring her home?

Gari needed to come down with a major illness. Something nearly but not totally fatal. That would be difficult to pull off, though, because she was a clumsy liar, a fact that Tandi had pointed out to her might be a bit of a problem in getting a boyfriend. Let Tandi tell Jaiden he smelled nice when he stunk like a shoe left in the rain. She wasn't any good at pretending; she was into *Planning. Executing. Winning.*

But how did you do that when your opponent was the whole U.S. Army, and an entire U.S. Air Force base surrounded you? When even a minor fender bender near the front gate was reported in the paper?

She got out of bed and felt her way in the semidark through the kitchen to the den. Indy followed her. Gari booted up the computer, blinking as the screen flared light into the room. There was an e-mail from her mom.

Hi, Sweetie,

Greetings from the Expeditionary Medical Group in Balad, Iraq! (That's the joint forces hospital. We have people from the Army, Navy, Air Force, and Marines here.)

Sandstorm the day I arrived. You know what the female troops call it? Free facials! Ha!

I want to call you, but there's only one phone we are allowed to call out from, and I haven't been able to stand in line long enough to use it. We'll have to use e-mail for now. How is North Carolina? Are you and Bo hitting it off?

There's a possibility I may get to go on a FOB tour soon. I'll send pictures. You send pictures too. Don't forget!

Love you all the time,
Mom

What time was it in Iraq? She couldn't think. What was a FOB? Army talk, she guessed. Gari typed back:

Hi, Mom,
I'm here. I'm okay except that my stomach hurts. Bo's dog is nice.

She put her head down next to the keyboard. Indy curled up, a pleasant circle of fur and warmth, on top of her bare feet. How could she describe the last two days without lying?

She fell asleep with her glasses on. The sky outside grayed into morning. On the nightstand in her new room, the little green figure stood watch where she'd left him.

16
STEP ONE

Over the weekend, Bo wished he'd taken his dad's advice and written out a list of how to be nice to Gari, because she wasn't making it easy. She didn't want to watch the University of Tennessee game on TV with them or wear his orange football jersey, even though he'd taken it off and offered it to her at halftime. She wasn't interested in the new ramps at the skateboard park, and she read every label on every can of food in their house to see if there was a trace of animal in it. She hijacked the computer, and she took showers that lasted way more than three minutes. She said *of course* she was going to the air show . . . what, did he think she was planning to run away or something? And she started feeding Indy baby carrots, which the dog snapped up like they were better than bologna.

Worse, she continued to ruin his life at school on Monday. The day began with this announcement:

"Staff, the School Commission will visit THIS FRIDAY. I have NOT received the majority of the assessment reports. They are NOT complete until I receive them IN the office. I must have ample time to compile a master report. Students: I expect YOU to be on your BEST behavior."

Bo knew that meant HIM.

Miss Loupe said, "Thank you, class, for helping me finish our report despite all that . . . that . . . chaos on Friday." She avoided looking at Bo.

He'd missed moving the Ugly, Ugly Couch to the library too. Because of Gari, all he'd done last Friday afternoon was sit in detention in the principal's office.

Then, in case somebody, somewhere, didn't know that Gari existed, Miss Loupe invited her to introduce herself.

"You don't have to come up front, but stand so we can hear you." She smiled encouragingly at Gari.

Gari pushed herself to her feet, gripping her desk. She was across the room from Bo, to the far left. As she took a breath, he saw her finger find the deep groove that Dillon had left behind. Bo realized that with her replacing Dillon, there were now more girls than boys in the class. Now they'd *always* be outvoted.

Most of the class had turned to look at Gari. Their faces swirled together in one blurry mass. Gari tucked her hands into her pockets so no one could see them shaking. Her mom always coached her: "Keep it short. Keep it simple. Breathe."

She focused on a chipped spot on her desk.

"I'm Gari Whaley. I live in Seattle. Well, I used to live in Seattle. I like art. I don't eat meat. My mom is in Iraq, and she's in the Army."

She started to dive back into her seat, but Zac asked, "How come you have a boy name?"

Gari sighed. "There's an *i* at the end. It's short for Garrison. It's a fort, you know, like the Alamo?"

Allison raised her hand. "Is it true that Bo's name is really Bogart?"

There was a silence, followed by Aimee's barely controlled giggling. Gari saw her chance and sat down.

"Bogart, as in Humphrey Bogart?" Miss Loupe said to Bo.

He could barely nod. After Friday, Miss Loupe was going to pile on him too, wasn't she? But Miss Loupe's gaze didn't stay on him long. She came to stand in front of Allison.

". . . Bogart, as in the Oscar-winning actor who also served in the Navy, and as legend has it, had his lip split open by the shackles of a prisoner he was escorting, but still managed to chase the guy down and turn him over to the police?"

Cool, Bo thought. *Cool. Much cooler than Paris.*

". . . Bogart, the guy who played chess by mail with GIs in World War II? Bogart, the actor who was known for playing tough, smart, and funny characters, and who is ranked number one on the American Film Institute's list of greatest screen actors?"

Allison shifted in her seat and glanced over at Aimee. Aimee was looking at Miss Loupe. Listening to Miss Loupe.

Then Miss Loupe turned back to Gari.

"Thank you for introducing yourself. I respect your bravery in allowing your mom to serve. I have a brother in Afghanistan. We've started a care box for him." She indicated the box that sat at the base of her desk. "We can start one for your mom too."

"No, thank you," said Gari. She folded her arms.

"Well, then . . ." Miss Loupe cleared her throat. She picked up a thick black marker and briskly crossed the room to stand by a piece of poster board mounted to the wall inside the doorway. "I'd like to seize this moment for my casting call."

At the top of the poster board she wrote:

THE UGLY COUCH PLAYERS
"SAY YES, AND . . ."

She paused. "Gari, I know you haven't met our namesake, the Ugly, Ugly Couch, yet —"

"Oh, yes," said Gari. "I did. It smells like bagel chips."

"Tortilla chips," said Trey.

"Whatever," said Gari.

"In any case," said Miss Loupe. "We're starting an improvisational theater group, and the couch is part of the fun. But we'll all learn more about it over the next few weeks."

She turned, and with a great flourish, wrote her name on the poster board. The marker squeaked as she rounded the cursive capital L in her name and again when she dashed off the last e.

"There!" She faced the class and twirled the marker through her fingers. "Who would like to add their name next?" She stopped twirling and met Bo's eye. She prepared to send the marker flying over several rows of seats to him.

Bo wanted to. He wanted to so much that he could feel his legs readying to lift him out of his chair and through the Taped Space to Miss Loupe. He could see himself writing his name, the swift downstroke of the B, then the double bounce of the sideways curves, followed by one quick round swipe of the o. The marker would give off a sweet smell and there would be shiny dark spots at the joints of the letters until the ink dried.

But . . .

If he put his name on the list, wasn't he as good as saying he wanted to be here next summer? The only way that would happen was if his dad was NOT here.

He'd heard his dad call the Middle East "the sandbox." But it wasn't play. It was for real. It might even be a sand trap.

Miss Loupe was walking forward, her hand swinging back to toss the marker. Bo's fingers itched to catch it.

But he shook his head. *No.*

He couldn't put his name on that list. It felt too much like planning to not eat pickles with his dad for a whole year. An un-erasable mistake.

Miss Loupe's smile stuck in place. Her arm stopped its forward motion so suddenly that the marker nearly dropped to the floor. Bo looked down at his desk.

Miss Loupe swallowed and then lifted her chin an inch. She looked away from Bo to the rest of the class. "Anyone?"

"Why not?" said Rick. He got up, took the marker, and signed his name.

"Me too," said Melissa, closing her notebook and getting in line behind him.

Shaunelle signed. So did Sanjay. Zac. Kylie.

"Maybe I should see about getting an agent," said Allison as she signed.

Aimee followed Allison, the A's in their names lining up. Martina was close behind.

118

"Trey?" Miss Loupe said. "How about you? We could use an artist to design programs and promo material."

Trey glanced at Bo, who was intently shredding a corner of his Student Handbook. Trey shrugged, got up, and put his name on the list.

In the end, most of Room 208 joined the Ugly Couch Players. Miss Loupe taped the marker to the side of the poster board. She regarded the list and squared her shoulders.

"Thank you for your support," she said to the class. "I didn't mean to pressure any of you. You don't have to decide today, and, of course, my first job is to be your classroom teacher."

Bo could hear her feet padding quietly back to her desk. He finally dared to look up. Miss Loupe was nearly hidden behind her books and papers. But he could see that she was holding the framed quote Marc had given her. Was she thinking Bo was the biggest crack in her classroom?

While everyone signed that stupid list, Gari had been thinking about Plan B. She had the torn paperback page from her mom's book hidden under her binder. She edged out the rectangle of paper and wrote:

1. Recruit some supporters.

That was always the first step in any campaign.

But who? Who would help her? Everyone here loved the Air Force. She'd seen the yellow ribbons and the bumper stickers. She guessed that meant they loved the Army too.

At lunch, she ignored the other girls and placed her little army figure on the table, lining him up along the crack that ran from one side to the other. She knelt down beside the table until she was eye level with the soldier.

Click. Flash. Crank.

She shook a few stars out of her plastic bag. They settled around him.

Click. Flash. Crank.

"Hey," said Shaunelle. "Where did you get those stars?"

Gari looked out from behind her camera. "I made them. I can show you with a straw wrapper."

"Weird," Aimee said.

"With a capital W," Martina agreed. She blew on her soup to cool it.

"Anybody, like, *normal*, want an Oreo?" said Allison. She passed cookies to every girl but Gari and Shaunelle.

Shaunelle looked at her crumpled straw wrapper. "Later, okay?" she said to Gari. She opened her new mystery book and began to read while she sipped her chocolate milk.

Gari put away her camera. Why would her mom want pictures of a plastic soldier? She wished she could recruit thousands of supporters as easily as she could make stars. Then she could launch an attack on . . . well . . . everybody.

After school, there was an e-mail from her mom:

Honey, don't worry.

FOBs are Forward Operating Bases throughout Iraq. Some medical staff work there, instead of here at the main hospital. I'll only be out in the field for a few days as part of my orientation. It's not that dangerous, and it's important for me to see how my patients are cared for before they arrive here. It's like a chain — every link is important.

Gari turned off the computer and went to the only store she could walk to. Her mom was changing their plan by leaving the safe area. Fine. Gari would change her plan too. Minutes later, she exited the Base Exchange with a shopping bag. When she got home, she checked off step one:

1. Recruit some supporters.

Below it, she added step two:

2. Decide what they should do.

That was the tough part. What would make her mom come home? Not her careful plans to stay with Tandi. Not a fake illness. But maybe trouble would.

17
IN CIRCLES

On Tuesday, Miss Loupe didn't mention the Ugly Couch Players sign-up again. Instead, she introduced a math game. She held up a small blue rubber ball.

"Have you ever played pinball?"

Half the class raised their hands.

"Good," said Miss Loupe. "Then you know that the object is to keep the ball moving and think on your feet. Bo, Gari, would you come up and be my two pinball flippers?"

Inside the Taped Space, Bo and Gari stood as far away as possible from each other.

"Now," said Miss Loupe. "How many people in the class?"

"Twenty-eight," said Melissa.

Miss Loupe wrote *28* on Gari's side of the chalkboard and *28* on Bo's.

"How many girls?"

"Four — oh, wait . . . fifteen!" said Melissa again.

Miss Loupe wrote *15* above Gari's number 28 and drew a horizontal line between them, making the fraction $\frac{15}{28}$.

"How many boys?"

"Thirteen," said Zac.

Miss Loupe made the fraction $\frac{13}{28}$ on Bo's side.

"So, if a pinball were to bounce off Gari or Bo and into the rest of the class, what is the chance that it would hit a boy?"

Kylie raised her hand. "Can we use a calculator?"

Miss Loupe nodded.

"Thirteen minus one is twelve, which divided by twenty-eight is point four two nine. Almost forty-three percent," Kylie sang out.

"Good!" Miss Loupe tossed the ball to Bo. "Let's try another one. But now, the game is to try to keep the ball going by finding someone who has something in common with you. Bo, name something you like."

"Pogo sticks," said Bo.

"How many of you own a pogo stick?" said Miss Loupe.

No one raised a hand.

Miss Loupe wrote $\frac{1}{28}$ on the board. Four percent. She took the ball from Bo and handed it to Gari.

Gari wanted to sit down. She picked something she knew everyone here hated.

"Vegetarians."

Aimee poked Allison. "That's you! You eat carrots and Oreos! No meat! That's you! Raise your —"

Allison reluctantly raised her hand.

$\frac{2}{28}$, Miss Loupe wrote. .07. Seven percent.

She instructed Gari to toss the ball to Allison.

"Now, Allison, your turn. Bonus points if your answer can make the ball bounce back to your flipper here." She patted Gari on the shoulder.

"Green," said Allison, noting Gari's shirt.

Lots of kids raised their hands, including Gari. Miss Loupe gave three bonus points to the girls' team. The ball bounced to Gari and then from one green lover to the next. Rick yelled out the answer: $\frac{18}{28}$. Sixty-four percent.

Miss Loupe awarded five points to the boys' side for that.

The ball ricocheted around the room to shouts of "Hey! I didn't know *you* liked tree frogs . . . the Miami Dolphins . . . hot sauce . . . pink hair . . . NASCAR . . . high dives . . ." Eventually, the girls won, but only by eleven points, which was, as Rick pointed out, only two percent more than the boys' score.

Worse than that, Bo had fun. When the math lesson was over, he couldn't help it. He glanced over at the Ugly Couch Players cast list. What were the chances that he would ever get a teacher like this again? Zero.

He should ask his dad. Ask him what the chances were of that assignment going through. Of Bo getting to stay. Of his dad having to go. Maybe everything would equal out.

Bo did his probability homework at the kitchen counter that night. His dad had to go to an Airmen's Leadership School banquet and give a speech. Bo's mom went with him. They were on base, a stone's throw away, so they let Bo and Gari stay home together.

"Want to check our answers?" he asked Gari. "I think I got them all right."

"Nope."

Gari went into her room and added to her plan:

3. Make sure you have a high probability of being heard!

On Wednesday, Mrs. Heard announced that the library and the construction of the Reading Castle would be a special focus of the School Commission visit.

"Everything must be PERFECT!" Mrs. Heard said.

She sent Bo and Trey to the library to move the Ugly, Ugly Couch once again. The two of them pushed and shoved it down the hall to the cafeteria, where Mrs. Purdy reluctantly agreed to house it in one blocked-off corner, along with cans of paint and extra lumber.

"Come back for it as soon as they leave on Friday," she said, arranging a blanket over the whole mess.

As they walked back, Trey said, "You aren't going to join the Players?"

"We're moving," said Bo.

"I know," said Trey. "Me too. Sometime. But I'm doing it. You're ten times better than me."

"Why bother?" said Bo.

"It's better than last year."

"What is?"

"School."

"Who *are* you?" Bo grabbed Trey by the shoulders and butted his head into Trey's forehead.

"Ow." Trey backed off, laughing.

"Just checking," said Bo. "They left your skull, but they did a good job removing your brain."

If he did stay for another year and moved off base, would Trey still be his friend? There were two middle schools, one close in and one farther out. What if they ended up at different ones?

On Thursday, Miss Loupe reminded them that she was mailing the care box to Marc the next day. If they had anything to add to it, they should bring it in tomorrow. And then she began the next math lesson: the formula for the circumference of a circle.

Gari already knew how to find circumference. She'd learned it last year. Besides, she was trying to STOP her mind from racing around in circles. She stuck the sketch she was working on inside her math book.

She had a plan now, Plan B, and it didn't require her to say one word. But it would be dramatic, and powerful, and it would change the way people thought. She had supporters. She knew what they would do. And she knew on which day she would have a high probability of being heard.

She quietly slid her plastic bag nearly half-full of stars from her backpack. Underneath her desk, she folded star after star, adding them to the bag, trying to keep her mind cool, calm, and focused. Until the School Commission visit tomorrow.

18
ARRANGING OBJECTS

Friday morning was easier than Gari thought it would be. It turned out that vomiting on your first day at school made everyone believe you when you said you needed to be excused *now*. And no one checked to see *which* bathroom she'd run to.

The bathroom on the kindergarten hall was marked with a handmade sign: OUT OF ORDER. Gari pushed against the darkened wood of the door and slipped inside. The smell of sewage was so thick that she had to pull her T-shirt over her nose. She opened her backpack, which was full of supplies. She'd bought five bags of army men from the BX. Later, she'd gone back for red paint. Black crayons. Super Glue. She took one last look at the sketch she'd made, and then she began to work, quickly and smoothly, on her campaign to bring her mom home.

When she finished, she looked over the scene she had created. Piles of little green figures, some of them on their sides, lay all over the floor. The sinks were filled with stagnant puddles of red paint. She'd taken a black crayon and written one word on each of the three mirrors:

BRING THEM HOME!

In the stalls, she'd filled each toilet with more red paint, and flushed one with paper towels in it to make it overflow. It wasn't exactly like the picture of the antiwar rally, but it was close. And she hoped it might cause a lot of trouble. She picked up the black crayon again and wrote GARI WHALEY in the corner of the right-hand mirror, just to be sure.

She slipped out of the bathroom and walked back to the library, where her stack of books was still waiting for her on Miss Candy's desk.

"Feeling better?" said Miss Candy, offering her a butterscotch drop.

"Hey," said Shaunelle, who was gathering up her books too. "Can you still show me how to make those stars?"

"Later," said Gari. "We should get to class."

Knock, knock.

Mrs. Heard opened the door and put her head inside Room 208. All of Miss Loupe's class was diligently completing the math problem she'd written on the board. Heads were bowed over papers, and the only sound was the *scritch, scritch* of pencils.

"Miss Loupe, the Commission has arrived. Since your classroom had the most extensive report on its physical condition . . ." She smiled at Miss Loupe. "I thought we'd start here."

Mrs. Heard stepped to the side, and three people walked into

Room 208: a woman so skinny she would have been able to slide under the door if it hadn't opened, another woman in a white pantsuit, and one man, with no hair on his head but sideburns that stretched deep into his cheeks. Each of them had a clipboard, and the pantsuited woman had a palm-sized gadget that she tapped at with a plastic pen the instant she moved into the classroom.

She examined the chalkboard on which Miss Loupe had written the math problems for the day. There was a crack running through it. *Tap, tap, tap.*

She bent down to view a spot where the baseboard had slightly detached from the floor. *Tap, tap.*

She looked up at the bent cage that covered the clock. *Tap, tappity-tap.*

The other two members of the Commission didn't move around at all. They flipped pages on their clipboards back and forth and occasionally whispered to each other. The skinny woman pointed to one of Miss Loupe's signs. The man nodded.

Mrs. Heard stood at the door, watching and waiting.

"Thank you," said the woman with the gadget. "We've seen what we need."

Mrs. Heard moved to open the door for them to leave.

"But," said the man, holding his clipboard against his chest, "I still believe it's the quality of the teaching that matters, not the condition of the classrooms. We can spend all the money we want on repairing infinitesimal cracks, but if the teachers aren't doing their jobs . . ."

129

Mrs. Heard's smile faded. "I don't believe that's a problem in my school," she said, fixing the man with a cool gaze. She swept her hand over the students of Room 208, who were the model of an industrious classroom.

"Oh, yes, they are *busy*," said the man, his sideburns bristling away from his face. "But what are they *learning*?" He indicated the quote on the wall:

ART IS ARRANGING OBJECTS TO CREATE BEAUTY

"The last time I checked, that was NOT part of the sixth-grade curriculum."

Mrs. Heard straightened the cuffs of her blouse, pulling them firmly out of the ends of her suit sleeves. They had embroidered flowers on them. "You don't believe in beauty, Mr. Johnson?"

"Not at the expense of facts," he said, walking over to Gari's desk. "This young lady has only been pretending to work that math problem. In reality, she has been making *these*." He reached under her desk and pulled out a plastic bag filled with paper stars.

Gari felt hot and cold at the same time. This wasn't the trouble she'd planned for.

Miss Loupe moved beside Gari and put her hand firmly on Gari's desk. She drew herself up as tall as possible.

"Mr. Johnson," she said, "with all due respect, Gari is my newest pupil. She joined the class last week. I'd like to give her time to adapt."

Mr. Johnson clipped Gari's bag of stars to the metal hinge at the top of his board. "Then perhaps you have another student who can explain how these quotes tie into the curriculum established by the state and approved by the school board?"

Miss Loupe turned to Melissa. "Would you show Mr. Johnson your notes, please?"

Melissa handed over her notebook. Mr. Johnson paged through the tabs marked Social Studies, Math, and Language Arts. Filed under each tab were lines of careful, color-coded, orderly notes, on everything from ecosystems to area and circumference to a list of their required reading. Melissa tried not to look smug, but she felt a pleased glow building in her cheeks.

Then Mr. Johnson came to the tab marked Taped Space, and he paused. He began to read intently. His eyes stopped midway down one page and he motioned his fellow Commission members to come closer.

"What's this?" he said, thumping his finger against the page. The three of them huddled over a certain paragraph.

"May I see?" said Mrs. Heard. "I'm afraid I can't address something if I don't know what you're talking about."

He shoved the notebook in front of Mrs. Heard. "Would you care to explain why one of your teachers is 'jumping on couches' and 'rolling on the floor' and encouraging this student to . . . to . . ." He spit out the words. ". . . 'just do the first thing that pops into her head'?"

Melissa let out a hiccup of fear.

"Those aren't Mrs. Heard's ideas," said Miss Loupe. She stood straight, her arms at her sides and her shoulders pushed back. She could have been standing at attention at any military ceremony. "They're mine."

"But Mrs. Heard hired you, did she not? She knows what's going on in your classroom, is that not so? Are you saying that Mrs. Heard has *approved* these ideas as acceptable teaching practice? Or are you saying that the principal doesn't have control of this school?"

The man with the sideburns looked at Miss Loupe as if she were a little mouse. Mrs. Heard was looking at her too. Miss Loupe looked from Melissa's notebook to Mr. Johnson to her former teacher, struggling to find the right words. There was a moment of horrible quiet.

Bo did the only thing he could think of. He bolted for the jammed window. He banged and pushed and threw his body against the stubborn frame. Everyone in Room 208, including all three members of the School Commission and Mrs. Heard, turned to look at him as though he had yanked them on a cord.

"What if this room caught on fire?" Bo said, jumping and twisting as if there were flames licking at his feet. He tried to smell the smoke, feel the heat. His voice rose. "What if the door were blocked and we couldn't get out? What if this window were the only way to save us and you hadn't fixed it . . . ?"

He wasn't nearly as good as Miss Loupe was at getting an audience to imagine a scene. The woman with the gadget was staring down at the floor. The other woman looked as if she would rather be at a dentist's appointment. Mr. Johnson's side-burns twitched.

The alarm! The alarm! The alarm needs to go off! Right now!
It didn't.

But Shaunelle raised her hand and said, "Yes, and what if we tried to break open that window and got cut on the glass?"

Rick said, "Yes, and I broke my arm as I fell out the other side?"

Trey said, "Yes, and what if Allison here . . ." He indicated Allison to the Commission members. ". . . *croaked* from breathing all that smoke while she was waiting to leap out the window, and her mom and dad sued?"

Allison's eyes widened at the thought of her own tragic death. She said, "Yes, and . . . they would. Totally."

"Yes, and it's not only here," said Aimee. "There are loose tiles in the hallway, and all over the school. Someone is going to trip and bust their head open."

One by one, the members of Room 208 listed every crack they had discovered.

"Yes, and in the girls' room . . ."

"Yes, and on the playground. . . ."

"Yes, and you wouldn't believe how bad . . ."

Even Gari entered the skirmish, to Bo's surprise. Eyeing her bag of stars, still pinched in Mr. Johnson's grasp, she contributed:

"Yeah, and there's a bathroom in the kindergarten hall that would completely flunk the health code. My mother is a nurse, so I should know."

Tappity tap. Tappity-tappity-tappity tap. At least one person on the Committee was listening. The other two seemed overwhelmed by the torrent of information pouring over them.

Before they could recover, Mrs. Heard reached for Melissa's notebook.

"I'll take care of this, don't you worry," she told Mr. Johnson. "We have important things to focus on, as you have heard. Now, the library?" Her large arms shepherded the Commission members out of Room 208. As she shooed them through the door, she turned and deftly handed the notebook to Miss Loupe. They looked at each other for a moment. Then Mrs. Heard was gone.

Miss Loupe slowly walked backward from the door, as if she expected it to reopen at any moment. She shuffled into the middle of the Taped Space and looked down at the browning edges of her tape, then up at her class.

A huge smile broke over her face.

"Brilliant!" she said. "The best piece of improvisational theater I've seen in a long time!" She ran her fingers through her hair, sending her spikes even higher. "Wait until I tell Marc about this!"

She stopped smiling when she saw that Melissa had her head down on her desk. Miss Loupe put her hand on Melissa's shoulder. "You didn't do anything wrong," she said.

Melissa raised her head and pushed her bangs out of her eyes.

Miss Loupe continued, "I'll tell Mrs. Heard that I can explain how everything in this notebook relates to our curriculum and more." She handed Melissa back her notebook. Melissa put both of her hands on top of it and folded them.

Bo was still standing by the window.

"Does that really not open?" Miss Loupe said, a frown forming.

Bo banged his fist against the frame, which loosened the crooked seal of dried paint. He pushed the sash up and a gust of air blew into the classroom. He peered into the sill. Just as he thought: bugs, piles of them, legs and antennae and crunchy wings. He hoped none of the School Commission would run into his dad.

"Are you sure you don't want to join the Ugly Couch Players?" Miss Loupe said to Bo.

Bo swooshed across the room as if he were on skis. He picked up the marker. He signed his name with quick, dark strokes: *BO*. Not Bogart, not yet. Just Bo. But just Bo was pretty good.

"And Gari!" said Miss Loupe. "You're a natural! You've had hardly any training and yet you jumped in there! Bravo!"

Gari gave a quick smile, her first all week. Before she could say a thing, Bo had inked in her name, under his.

No! she thought. *You're the show-off, not me! To stand up in front of all those people!*

She shook her head at Bo, motioning for him to strike through her name, but he ignored her.

135

Well, it didn't matter, because as soon as the School Commission got to that bathroom . . .

It didn't take long. Twenty minutes later . . .

Knock, knock, knock.

Mrs. Heard was back to see Room 208, but this time, her face was dark, as serious as a heart attack, as Gari's mom would say. She motioned Miss Loupe to the door. She said something to her in a low voice and handed her a slip of paper.

The class started whispering.

Melissa steadied herself.

Gari steadied herself.

Miss Loupe clutched the oval that hung around her neck. The cord holding it broke, but she didn't notice. She looked at her class and then at the piece of paper.

"Go," Mrs. Heard said in a tight voice. "I've told the School Commission to come back another time. I'll take over your class."

What? thought Gari. *Don't they know it was me? MY idea?*

They can't get her in trouble over the Taped Space! thought Bo.

Melissa was so scared she couldn't think.

Mrs. Heard took Miss Loupe by the shoulders and gave her a tiny but firm shake. "Carol! GO!"

Miss Loupe ran out the door, down the hallway, out the side door, through the grass, and into the teachers' parking lot.

As she ran, the cord and oval fell through her peacock-green shirt and onto the ground.

"Sixth graders," Mrs. Heard announced. "I'll be your teacher for the remainder of the day." She moved into the room and stood behind Miss Loupe's desk.

"Why, ma'am?" Melissa finally spoke up in a small voice. "What's happened, ma'am?"

"Miss Loupe has had an emergency come up." Mrs. Heard unbuttoned and re-buttoned the top jeweled fastener on her suit jacket.

"It's all my fault, ma'am!" Melissa burst out. "Please don't blame Miss Loupe!"

Mrs. Heard's voice was quieter than Bo had ever heard it. "Melissa, please calm down," she said. "It's not about that. She would have told you if . . ." She paused. Then into the silence, she said:

"It's Miss Loupe's brother. His unit in Afghanistan reported him missing."

The class erupted.

"Marc! He sat on our couch! . . . The Super Bowl . . . Remember, the cat ate his salsa . . . I can't believe he . . . his box is still . . . Army . . . missing . . . Does that mean . . . He's dead?"

Gari sat in the middle of the chaos, not saying a word. She squeezed the one little green army figure still in her pocket. She didn't know much about Marc, not like the rest of the class.

He'll be okay, thought Gari. *He'll be okay. He has to be.*

But the words in her head couldn't drown out the other words in there too. The ones that had popped into her head like huge splotches of red paint when she'd heard the words *Army* and *missing* and *dead*:

It will feel like this. When it happens to me, it will feel like this.

19
OUT OF THE PICTURE

The weekend, for once, felt too long.

On Saturday, Trey asked Bo to go to the skate park, and they dropped in the steepest side, over and over, until their legs and ankles hurt. They asked Gari too, because Bo knew his dad would want them to, but she refused to come. Instead, she went to the BX and bought the last bag of little green army men.

Bo's mom made macaroni and cheese for dinner, a giant casserole's worth, with toasted crumbs on top, the kind she used to make before she became a P.E. teacher and lost fifty pounds. She made an extra casserole and placed it in the freezer.

"Just in case," she said.

Gari ate two bites and went to check her e-mail.

Hi, baby. Only have a minute. Crazy busy here. My FOB trip was approved, so I have to prep for that. Plus a million other things.

Is everything okay? You haven't been writing much. I'll try to call soon.

All the time,

Mom

P.S. Have you taken any pictures yet?

While Gari was on the computer, Bo sneaked into her room and borrowed the mouthpiece off her trumpet. He didn't feel bad because she hadn't even picked it up since she'd gotten there, not even when he'd asked her if she could play it. When Taps sounded that night, he tried not to think about when he'd heard it in movies: at funerals. He put the mouthpiece to his lips and acted as if he were a magnificent trumpet player.

On Sunday, after church, Gari tried to reach Tandi. She wasn't home. Gari got a new plastic bag and sat on her bed and folded star after star after star. She wasn't folding them for Tandi anymore. She was folding them because if she didn't, those awful paint splotches of words filled her head. Even after an afternoon of folding, the bag still looked empty.

Bo's dad made confidential phone calls to his contacts in the Army, but no one knew more than the initial report about Marc. Or they weren't saying.

Indy ate a small hole in the hallway carpet and a large one in the toe of a black shoe that she found in Bo's room.

Gari stared at her new bag of army men and thought of the others she'd left in the bathroom. If someone found them now, without the publicity of the School Commission visit, her message wouldn't get farther than the principal's office.

Mrs. Heard called Miss Loupe at her apartment six times, but got no answer.

20
I DON'T KNOW,
BUT I'VE BEEN TOLD . . .

Miss Loupe did not return on Monday.

Bo hated the substitute teacher that Mrs. Heard hired. She wore shoes that clicked loudly on the floor and only one pair of earrings, and she was tall. Bo didn't listen to anything she said. He didn't answer when she asked questions. He stared at his name near the bottom of the list of the Ugly Couch Players and tried to remember how good it had felt to put it there. Miss Loupe's name was first on that list. What were the chances that she would come back?

On Tuesday, Kylie forgot her sash for Safety Patrol. Melissa broke three pencils, and Zac started an argument with Sanjay over who got to be first in line for lunch. Shaunelle tried to straighten one of Miss Loupe's posters, but instead made it fall off the wall. The substitute reviewed probability concepts for the scheduled math test, but Room 208 got so many answers wrong that she decided to postpone it.

And so, on Wednesday, five days after the news about Marc, the Ugly, Ugly Couch still sat in one corner of the Young Oaks cafeteria, wedged between a stack of plywood and two sealed cans of Stone Gray paint. Several musty boxes of Student Hand-books were piled onto its cushions, and the plaid woolen blanket Mrs. Purdy had thrown over it camouflaged the whole mess. Even the couch's odor was masked by the thick smell of beef chili and the highly unusual scent of freshly baked cornbread. Only a stray roll of masking tape betrayed the couch's presence, by lift-ing the edge of the blanket enough to reveal one of its heavy brass feet.

Near this carefully concealed mound, Room 208 had claimed the same two lunch tables it always did: one for the boys and one for the girls.

At the boys' table, Bo sniffed his watery chili. *Yuck.* He should open his chocolate milk first. He tapped his straw on the table to loosen its wrapper and thought of Miss Loupe, rowing and chant-ing to her own beat. And Marc, who had probably sung jody calls in basic training. He felt itchy inside.

"I don't know, but I've been told . . ." he said loudly.

He pointed the still-wrapped straw at Sanjay, who was sitting across from him.

Sanjay looked surprised at the challenge. "Uh . . . You stop running . . . uh . . ." He shrugged. ". . . your boots will mold?"

"Lame," Bo said. He jabbed the straw at Zac, who was sitting in Dillon's old seat, and chanted again: "I don't know, but I've been told . . ."

Zac said without thinking, "Generals' butts are made of gold!"

"Whooo! Yeah!" Rick yelled. Then he looked apologetically over at Bo. "Sorry."

"He's a colonel, not a general," said Bo.

"He will be," said Rick.

An announcement crackled over the school's PA system:

"Students, staff: Excuse the interruption, please. The School Commission's return visit, which was scheduled for this afternoon, has been postponed."

"I knew it," said Allison. She opened her lunch bag. Carrots and cookies. "They're *never* coming back! They should put somebody who knows the right people on that Commission. Like me."

Melissa sprinkled her chili with crumbled cornbread, trying to make it thick enough to stay on her plastic fork. "Who cares about them? Why doesn't she announce when Miss Loupe is coming back? Or what's happening with Marc? Why doesn't anyone ever tell us what's going on?"

Gari ignored all of them. She wasn't eating anything. Instead, she arranged and rearranged her soldiers on the table in front of her.

Mrs. Heard was still talking:

". . . your cooperation in keeping Young Oaks neat and orderly. Unfortunately, the School Commission has not yet set a new date for their arrival, so I cannot tell you when to expect them. It may happen on short notice. Therefore, please keep up the good work. We want them to see that we take pride in our school, even as we seek its improvement."

Mrs. Purdy harrumphed. She had half a mind to take the cornbread muffins she had made from scratch for the School Commission and feed them to the birds on the playground.

The speaker crackled for a second, and then came back on:

"One last announcement: The base has informed me that the jet noise may be louder than usual all this week. The demonstration team is rehearsing for the air show this weekend. Remember to *beaaaar* with it!"

Bo sang out again: "I don't know, but I've been told . . ."

Trey beat back his reply: "Heard's not dead, she's just real old!"

The whole boys' table whooped with laughter, but at the word *dead*, Bo's itchiness came back. He lifted his straw in the air and blew off its wrapper at Sanjay. Sanjay snatched the wrapper, wadded it up, and surprised everybody by throwing it at the girls' table. It landed in Martina's chili.

Martina giggled, but Allison rolled her eyes in disgust. She swiped one of Gari's army men and lobbed it at Sanjay.

On the opposite side of the school, Mr. Nix's class paused in their construction of the giant card they were making. Red and white stripes (not quite parallel) covered a piece of poster board, except for the upper left corner, which was painted a solid blue. Each first grader, when instructed to do so by Mr. Nix, was taking a turn with the paper punch, clipping pairs of tightly spaced holes into the blue rectangle at regular intervals. A pile of fifty crisp yellow ribbons all cut to the same length lay ready to be threaded through the holes and tied into loops.

Mr. Nix supervised them closely: "Forty-seven . . . Don't make the holes too close! Forty-eight . . . That's good, nice and straight . . . Forty-nine . . ."

"I love it at the air show when the planes sneak up from behind and scare you!" one first grader said. She whooshed her hand over Tony's head as he took his turn with the hole punch.

"Fifty!" Mr. Nix surveyed his class. "Who knows what the fiftieth state to join the Union was?"

"Corn dogs!" a boy said, smacking his lips. "Funnel cakes! Barbecue! I'm going to eat everything!"

In the library, Miss Candy flicked the light switch in her storage room. Nothing happened. *Tuck Everlasting!* The light must have burned out. Where was the media cart? Mr. Nix had asked to show a movie this afternoon, and the cart was somewhere behind all the construction materials that had been stacked out of sight. Airman Kresge had helped her store most of the supplies in here for the School Commission visit, but now he wasn't available to help her take it all out. At least not until after the air show. The overflow had gone to the cafeteria, which Mrs. Purdy had grumbled about. Was *still* grumbling about.

The little green figure skimmed by Sanjay's head, bounced off Zac's cheek, and ricocheted into Bo's milk carton. The nearly full carton turned over and poured a pint of chocolate liquid onto Trey's lap.

"No one knows the fiftieth state?" Mr. Nix said.

"Who's this card for?" said Tony, who was still holding the paper punch. "I forget."

"Hawaii," Mr. Nix said. "H-A-W-A-I-I is the fiftieth state. Notice there are two A's and two I's."

Trey and Bo picked up their corn muffins —
"I don't know, but it's been said —"
— and threw them.
"Girls are dumb as pencil lead!"

In the dim light, Miss Candy bumped into a corner of the media cart. Ouch! She rubbed her bruised thigh and inspected the cart. Its shelves had been stacked with boxes and papers. She hurriedly shoved them off and pulled the movie Mr. Nix had requested from the closet shelf. She couldn't make it out in the dark, but it seemed to be a video about staying safe when you find yourself alone at home. It had come in last week; she hadn't had a chance to preview it. She put the video on the cart and edged toward the door.

A corn muffin hit Allison's bag of Oreos, dumping them onto the floor. She reached down and picked up several of the cookies —
"I don't know, but I've been told —"
— and handed them to her troops. They launched their ammunition high into the air.
"Boys smell worse than ten dead toads!"

"Hawaii?" Tony said. "This card is going to —"
"No, it's not going to Hawaii," Mr. Nix said. "Weren't you listening when I explained —"

Ca-click. Ca-click.

Mr. Nix reached for the paper punch, but it was too late. America now had a fifty-first state.

Corn muffins and cookies and army men flew in the air. Straws, milk cartons, a whole bowl of chili. The boys stood up on their chairs and pelted crackers down on the girls. The girls shot their carrot missiles at the boys' heads. Rick stepped from his chair up onto the boys' table, and it tilted over with a crash. Gari ducked and wove through the battlefield, trying to retrieve all her men. Trays flew in all directions. Chili mixed with chocolate milk, and the sticky liquid from canned peaches coated the floor. They were throwing and dodging and slipping and yelling until no one knew who was on which side anymore.

Miss Candy wheeled the cart down the hall. As she passed the cafeteria, Mrs. Purdy exploded from the double glass doors, her hands waving in the air.

"OUT!" she yelled. "I will not tolerate fights in MY cafeteria! March straight to Mrs. Heard's office. ALL OF YOU!!"

A small group of boys and girls from Miss Loupe's sixth-grade class stumbled out of the cafeteria. The girls broke into a run, so they could get to Mrs. Heard's office first and tell their side of the story.

Oh, Winn-Dixie, thought Miss Candy. *We're in for it now.*

Mr. Nix wondered if he could tape and paint over the extra pair of punched holes. Miss Loupe would think his class didn't know how many stars were on an American flag! Or worse, she would think he couldn't count! He removed the giant card from his students' reach, placing it on his desk.

Miss Candy tapped at his classroom door.

"Your movie, Mr. Nix," she said. "Keep the VCR as long as you like. No one else has asked for it today."

"Some cheap *Army* thing started it," Allison was telling Mrs. Heard. *"Hers."* She tossed her hair in Gari's direction and held up one of the little green men.

"Oh?" Mrs. Heard said. "Would you empty your pockets please, Gari?"

Silently, Gari emptied her pockets onto Mrs. Heard's desk. Little green soldiers covered the stacks of paper. She was glad she'd left her new bag of stars safe inside her desk in Room 208. Mrs. Heard might have flipped out seeing them again.

Mr. Nix put the video in the VCR.

"Class, this video will help you if you ever find yourself at home alone without your mother or your father or another responsible adult. Please pay attention to its important message about safety."

He pressed the play button and glanced at his watch. The video was about ten minutes long. That should be enough time to slip down the hall to see if there was more blue paint in the supply cabinet. . . .

* * *

"The rest of you, empty your pockets too!" Mrs. Heard commanded.

Sanjay had a ticket stub from a movie.

Melissa had a spool of dental floss.

Rick had a fake spider tattoo and wax for his braces.

Martina pulled out a movie ticket stub and a note from Sanjay, with a red ink heart on it.

Allison didn't have pockets in her skirt, so she leaned over to stare at Sanjay's note.

Aimee got the giggles. She tried and tried to stop, but she couldn't. Mrs. Heard told her to sit down and hold her breath.

Trey had a pencil stub and a half-finished picture of a school swarming with secret agents.

Zac had nothing but a ball of lint.

Bo produced one earplug, two golf balls, two bits of wadded-up tape, a worn strip of cloth with a key attached, and a mouthpiece. From a trumpet.

Gari stared at the mouthpiece and then stepped on Bo's foot, twisting her heel silently back and forth into his toes, below Mrs. Heard's line of sight.

When Miss Candy returned to the library, she tried to bring some order back to the storage closet. At least with the TV cart gone, she had space to turn around. She picked up a stapled packet of papers from the floor. The cover sheet was ripped and had a spot of gray paint on it. She tilted it toward the doorway, where there was more light.

"Assessment of the Physical Condition of My Classroom and the Surrounding Environment," she read.

She picked up another packet, shaking off the sawdust. It said the same thing.

Rhyme and Reason! What were Mrs. Heard's papers doing in her closet?

On the base, Airman Peters was high in the glass-enclosed top of the control tower. He could see the narrator for the demo team standing below him beside the runway, preparing to rehearse her voice-over for the air show. He radioed the single jet on the runway.

"Demo One, you are cleared for takeoff. Maintain at or below twenty-five thousand feet."

"Demo One is cleared for takeoff," confirmed the pilot.

In Mr. Nix's room, the class sat glued to their seats as, on the TV screen, a masked figure crept toward an oblivious babysitter who was eating popcorn on an ugly, ugly couch. The sound of a slightly out-of-tune piano tinkled in the back-ground.

Mrs. Heard picked up her phone to call the mothers and fathers of all the students standing before her in the office.

"I think my mom's not home now," Allison said. "I think she's, like, having lunch with the mayor."

Airman Peters watched the demo jet leap from the runway up into the brilliant fall sky, tucking its landing gear away as it rose.

It turned west, setting up for a low pass back over the airfield. The narrator on the ground addressed an imaginary crowd.

"Ladies and gentlemen," she said, allowing a pause for dramatic effect, "prepare for a startling demonstration of the F-15E's power, stealth, and speed. . . ."

In the cafeteria, Mrs. Purdy jerked open the door to the loading dock behind the lunchroom and hurled broken pieces of cookies and corn muffins into the Dumpster. Then she stood in the fresh air, pinching her two tiny cross earrings between her fingers and trying to breathe slowly. When she noticed the lone jet streaking toward the school, she automatically shifted her hands to cover her eardrums. About fifty feet away, in the deepening grass, was a loupe, but she couldn't see it.

Mr. Nix was hurrying back from the supply room with a can of blue spray paint. Far down the hallway, in his classroom, a TV screen filled with the image of blood-soaked couch cushions. Thirty-two first graders screamed. Mr. Nix was too far away; he didn't hear it.

Miss Candy sat on the floor of her dark storage closet, the shelves swaying around her. How was she going to explain to Mrs. Heard how all the missing assessments had turned into a pile of tattered and smudged paper in *her* library? What would she say to the teachers who had done the paperwork twice? She popped a butterscotch drop into her mouth. She could barely taste it.

* * *

BOOM! The demo jet screamed over Mrs. Purdy, then Mr. Nix, and then Miss Candy, all in a microsecond, before it streaked over Mrs. Heard's office, rattling her three tiny squares of windowpane and shaking clouds of dust from the ceiling tiles.

Gari dove to the floor at the blast of noise. Her head hit the edge of Mrs. Heard's desk, knocking her glasses off her face. At first, she went numb. Then Bo, followed by Trey, Rick, Sanjay, Zac, Allison, Melissa, Aimee, and Martina, laughed. Gari felt every bit of that.

Miles away, Miss Loupe held Nachos tightly in the living room of her parents' house. They all waited together.

And way, way on the other side of the world, the men of Operational Detachment Alpha 510 were searching for a missing member of their team. They couldn't find anything at all.

21
ONE OF YOU IS LEAVING

Bo's dad didn't speak for a full minute after they'd come inside the house. When he'd gotten Mrs. Heard's phone call to pick them up, he'd been at a meeting with the mayor of Reform, discussing last-minute details for security at the air show. He was still in his uniform, the dark blue pants and the light blue shirt that he wore when he wasn't flying. His command pilot wings and name tag were pinned above his pocket. His silver-trimmed blue flight cap was on the kitchen counter beside his car keys.

Bo stared at the long, red REMOVE BEFORE FLIGHT tag on his dad's tangle of keys. He listened to the clock above the stove tick from mark to mark. Gari was sitting at one of the tall counter chairs, a bag of ice pressed to her eye. Bo wished he'd asked for ice for his foot, where Gari had stomped on it.

"The girls' table started it," Bo finally said.

His dad held up a hand. "This is not about who started what. This is about why the two of you can't get along at school."

Indy, who was lying on the linoleum near her food dish, got up and slunk from the room.

"I thought it would be a good idea for Gari to be in the same class as you. I thought you would show her the ropes. I thought you would be the one person who would welcome her and make her feel at home here."

His dad paused before he thumped a stiff forefinger against the counter.

"You've already lost sight of the good thing I gave you to think about. But this is bigger than that. I'm telling you now that if there is one more incident like this, one more time when I hear of this kind of foolishness . . . one of you is leaving that classroom. And it won't be Gari."

"I don't care," said Gari. "I don't care which class I'm in."

"You've had way too much disruption already," said Bo's dad. "I won't move you. But Bo might do better in a classroom with more . . . structure."

"What?" said Bo. "What's that mean?"

"It means that I've heard complaints about Miss Loupe from the School Commission. It means that I've given her the benefit of the doubt, and I've hoped that you could handle yourself with such a young, inexperienced teacher. But maybe I was wrong."

"But she wasn't even there!" said Bo. "She's gone! Marc's gone! We have a stupid substitute who doesn't even —"

"It doesn't matter who's here and who's gone. I expect you to know what the right thing to do is and DO IT."

Bo's words broke out of the place where he'd tried to shut them in. "It does matter who's here! What if you aren't here? Mom said you might be leaving! She said they could send you to Afghanistan!"

Gari looked up and took the bag of ice away from her eye.

His dad sighed and leaned forward on the counter. He lowered his voice. "I might. I'll tell you as soon as I know something for sure."

"But you *want* to go! You want to say yes!" said Bo. "How come you always get to say YES, and I always have to say NO?"

He pulled his house key out of his pocket and ripped off the REMOVE BEFORE FLIGHT tag. He threw it on the counter. Gari jumped as it slid past her elbow.

"Fine. Who cares where I live? Who cares what I want to do? Who cares if the only thing that gets REMOVED is *me*?"

22
FOREIGN OBJECT DAMAGE

Mrs. Purdy was arguing with herself as she drove. She was on her way to the base air show, with a VIP ticket given to her by Colonel Whaley. The invitation had been hand delivered to her by Bo and Gari, along with their written apology for the food fight. Even though she had to drive by Young Oaks, she was not going in to the school. Why would she? It was Saturday. Today, she was invited to the guests-only lunch in the colonel's tent, catered by Hog Heaven. Today, she had a padded front-row seat for the Thunderbird show. Today, she hoped someone, somewhere, would get good news.

Yet she found herself slowing at the entrance to the school.

She shuddered at the memory of all those cornbread muffin crumbs, which were the same color as the yellowed linoleum floor. That spreading ocean of chocolate milk! And then yesterday, as she closed up for the day, she had tripped over a spinning roll of masking tape and nearly broken her foot.

She knew where it had come from. It had escaped from that horrible junk pile in her otherwise immaculate and well-ordered lunchroom. But why had she picked it up, and why was it still in her purse now, and why couldn't she stop thinking about it?

Mrs. Purdy and the roll of tape swerved into the school's parking lot and pulled up behind the cafeteria's loading dock.

At the air show, Bo plunged his hand into a tall plastic tub lined with a black garbage bag and filled with cubes of ice and dozens of cans of soda. Freezing water dripped from the cans as he handed them to a woman who struggled to keep two curly-headed kids seated in a double stroller.

"Two grapes, one orange," he said. "Six dollars."

He rubbed his knuckles against his shirt. They were bright red from the cold, and his fingers were going numb. He had known they would be pulling duty of some sort after the food fight, but this didn't seem fair. The line for drinks was getting longer every time he looked up, and worst of all, the booth his dad had assigned to him and Gari faced the rear of the flight line, as far away from show center as you could get. They could hear the announcer booming out introductions to the acts, but they couldn't see a thing.

Every other year, every other air show, he'd stood next to his dad and watched every single act, from start to finish.

"Come on, Gari. I'll be right back, I promise! I have to see the Flying Farmer. All you have to do is cover for me for a few minutes."

She ignored him, smiling sweetly at the next customer.

"Can I help *you*?" she said, emphasizing the word *you*, which clearly meant she wasn't going to help *him*.

Maybe she didn't understand.

"He looks like an old hick from the sticks," he said, eyeing the line and scooping out sodas as fast as he could. "You know, with torn overalls and a beat-up straw hat? He hobbles up to the plane with a cane and climbs in. Then, all of a sudden, WHOOSH! He 'accidentally' makes the plane *take off*!"

Bo put a can of soda through a burst of unexpected speed.

"He's zooming everywhere, pretending he doesn't know how to fly!"

He propelled the can into an out-of-control loop and a wild dive.

"The announcer is yelling at him to 'LAND! LAND!' but he can't, and he flips upside down and —"

Gari snatched the can from him and said to the man in front of their booth, "I'm sorry. He'll get you another soda that's not . . . *traumatized*."

Bo scooped out another soda and tried again.

"What if I trade you for time to see something else? Like the jet-powered outhouse? It shoots flames out the top!"

Gari collected two dollars for the soda. She thanked the customer warmly. She said nothing to Bo.

"Okay, I get that you're mad," he said. "But I have to see the Flying Farmer! And you have to take a turn with these freezing drinks. Look at my hands!"

"Yeah?" Gari said, turning on him and changing tactics. "Well, look at my forehead! Isn't it hilarious? Doesn't it make you want to *laugh*?"

A large purple bruise had spread above her glasses, from where her nose met her right eyebrow and up into her hairline.

There was an angry dent in the center where she had hit it on the corner of Mrs. Heard's desk.

"I didn't do that," Bo protested. "You did. It probably won't leave a scar. Not like what you gave me."

Gari gave him an incredulous look. "There's nothing wrong with your foot. I just stomped on it. A little."

Bo ignored the next customer in line and lifted his pant leg. "No, I'm talking about — Don't you remember giving me *this*?"

Gari stared at his hook-shaped scar.

"There was a big muddy lake with broken pine trees sticking out everywhere," she said slowly, remembering. "We were swimming, and then you said . . . you said there were giant, bloodthirsty, *girl-eating* lake sharks!" She pushed her glasses onto her nose and winced when they bumped her bruise. "I thought you meant it!"

"You grabbed that tree branch and sent me to the hospital!"

"I didn't know it had a fishing hook stuck in it! You were chomping your teeth and coming at me with one eye turned sideways! You were terrifying!"

"I was?" Bo felt strangely happy.

"Excuse me," said a woman wearing a floppy hat and carrying a red, white, and blue purse. "Can I get my drink? Sometime today?"

Bo wrapped a clean plastic grocery bag around his stinging hand and stuck it into the ice to get her a cherry soda.

"What were you doing with those toys at school anyway?"

"They aren't toys," Gari said. "They're pieces of *art*. But now, thanks to you and your whole stupid lunch table, they're officially 'weapons,' and Mrs. Heard has them locked up in her desk drawer!"

Mrs. Purdy entered the back of the cafeteria with her key. She opened her purse. The roll of tape lay there, nestled between her sunglasses and two tightly capped bottles of nail polish.

She sat down at one of the long tables, which smelled pleasantly of the lemon-scented ammonia with which she'd doused it. She tore off several small sections of the wide tape and pressed them lightly to the table. Uncapping one of the bottles of nail polish, she painted a single swipe of fluorescent color on half of the torn pieces. Then she recapped the bottle and screwed off the top of the second vial. She dipped the tiny brush into the glittery polish and gave each of the remaining blank pieces of tape a bold swipe of this contrasting color. Mrs. Purdy peeled each strip of tape from the table, and alternating colors as she went, carefully applied each piece to the back of one of the chairs surrounding the tables where Miss Loupe's class usually sat. That should do it!

Over the loudspeaker, the announcer broke into a yell of mock horror:

"Mr. Farmer, can you hear me? Sir! Sir! Turn the plane around! NO, NO! Not that way! SLOW DOWN! DO NOT TAKE OFF! DO NOT . . ."

Bo wiped his wet hands on his jeans. He had to see the Flying Farmer. Even if he couldn't stand next to his dad, they would at least be looking at the same sky.

He wiggled his stiff fingers into his back pocket and pulled out a green army figure.

"Mrs. Heard doesn't have this one."

"Where did you . . . ?" Gari squeezed her eyelids together briefly. "I mean, how did you . . . ?"

"OH, MY GOODNESS, FOLKS! HE'S IN THE AIR!" the announcer cried. "WATCH OUT FOR YOUR HATS! HOLD ON TO YOUR BABIES!"

"It's the one that started the fight," said Bo. "I picked it up off our table. But I still don't understand why you — "

Gari took it from his hand. The plastic figure was wearing a helmet, but no gun. Instead, it was carrying a medical kit.

"Five grape sodas and one diet, please," said a man, waving a twenty-dollar bill.

Gari pushed the army figure into her pocket. She reached around Bo into the tub of sodas. "Go," she told him.

Bo hesitated. He suddenly felt strange about leaving Gari to run the booth by herself. "Are you sure you can —"

Gari set three cans of soda on the ledge behind the counter, topped them with two more, and balanced the last one on the apex of her pyramid. She lifted the whole stack in one motion up over the booth's edge and into the customer's outstretched hands, plucking the twenty-dollar bill out of his grasp with the crook of one finger on the return.

As she swiftly counted back his change, the man nodded his approval. "You're as good as them gals at Hog Heaven!" He tipped her two dollars.

"Thanks, but it isn't heaven for hogs," Gari said to his back as he left the booth. She looked at Bo. "Why are you still here? Go see your stupid Flaming Farmer!"

Bo opened his mouth to correct her, and then closed it carefully. The announcer was saying in a voice of exaggerated calm: "Mr. Farmer. Mr. Farmer. We're going to talk you down. Can you hear me? MR. FARMER!"

Bo ran toward show center.

Mrs. Purdy smiled at her handiwork, which graced the circle of chairs surrounding each table. Girls would sit in the seats marked with neon pink, and boys would sit between them, in the ones marked with sparkly blue. They would all be responsible for making sure their mutual table was immaculate when they cleared their trays. She plunked the roll of sticky tape down in the middle of one of the tables. It would be ideal for picking up every last crumb from the floor.

All she had to do now was straighten the cover over that stack of junk — my goodness, half that ugly couch was visible! — and she could be off to the air show. How had the blanket slipped down?

But when she tugged at the corner of the woolen cloth, something under it moved. Mrs. Purdy froze. She had seen a rat in her lunchroom once, exactly six years and forty-eight days ago.

She wound her purse strap tighter about her wrist and peeled back the blanket.

An orange cat peered up at her.

"Nachos!" said a voice.

Mrs. Purdy turned to see Miss Loupe, who rushed past her and scooped up the cat from the couch. Miss Loupe's usually spiky hair was flat against her head. She had curved, dark half-moons under her eyes. She wore a gray sweatshirt that read AIR FORCE across the chest, and baggy gray pants that were many sizes too big for her.

"I'm sorry. I brought him to school with me," she said. "I didn't think anyone would be here, and then he got away, and I . . ." Her voice faded.

Mrs. Purdy, who was fighting the urge to shove Nachos and his thousands of puffy, shedding cat hairs out the back door, instead reached over and patted Miss Loupe's arm.

"Honey, honey, it's okay. When did you get back? Is there news?"

Miss Loupe sank down onto the arm of the Ugly, Ugly Couch and put Nachos on her lap. Her skin was blotchy around the edges of her cheeks. "Yes, there is."

She put one hand to her neck as if to hold on to something, but there was nothing there. She tightened her fist and kept going.

"They found Marc," she said.

Mrs. Purdy let out her breath louder than she meant to.

"He's alive," Miss Loupe said quickly. "But he — I don't know if I can — they won't —"

Miss Loupe looked past Mrs. Purdy to where a roll of tape was lying on a lunch table. Why was her tape in here? Why were there bits of tape on the backs of those chairs? She struggled to focus. She pulled Nachos up from her lap and squeezed him against her chest. He stretched out his bone-white front claws in protest. She tried again.

"He keeps calling for the rest of his team, and they . . ."

Miss Loupe fixed her eyes on the glossy enamel American flag that Mrs. Purdy had pinned to her stiffly pressed white collar.

"I shouldn't have left the Air Force. I shouldn't be a teacher," she said. "My dad was right. I shouldn't be safe, not when . . ."

Nachos didn't move as tears ran into his deep fur.

Mrs. Purdy set down her purse and wrapped her arms around Miss Loupe, puffy cat and all.

Hours and hours later, after the air show was over, and the military police had directed hundreds of souvenir-laden cars in slow-moving lines off the base, and the vendors had broken down their striped cloth tents, and the trash bags filled with sticky soda cans and torn foil burger wrappers had been carted away, and the planes had been secured, and the reporter for the *Reform Chronicle* submitted her article that estimated attendance at "up to 30,000 eager spectators," the final sweep of the flight line began.

Gari and Bo stayed for this too, because Colonel Whaley felt that a bit more Progress could be achieved with this last bit of Work.

"Mrs. Purdy would *love* to see us doing this," Bo said to Gari as they inched along, staring down at the ground. "I wonder why she didn't show up. She must still be mad."

They wore rubber gloves and held plastic bags. Their mission, along with the hundreds of troops standing shoulder to shoulder with them, was to inspect two miles of runway and two miles of taxiway for anything that could cause Foreign Object Damage.

"FOD," said Gari. "Sounds like a bad lunch."

Together, they found bits of metal, lots of twisted plastic straws, and a dead mouse. Gari found a bright red metal bolt.

"Oh, man, can I have that?" Airman Peters said. "I'll trade you a pack of gum for it. Slightly squished, but unopened." He offered the gum to her.

"No way," Airman Kresge said, plucking the bolt from Gari's hand. "I need it more than you do."

"The organizers place a few objects out here on purpose," explained Peters, still eyeing Gari's find. "To make us look carefully. If you find one, you get —"

He lurched for the red bolt, but Kresge closed his fist around it.

"A day off from work," he said. He grinned, placed the free pass into the shirt pocket of his fatigues, and buttoned it.

When they were finally done, Bo and Gari walked home. They walked past the curved domes of concrete hangars and the massive new brick-and-glass fire station and the well-lit base gym and the now-closed BX and the smaller shoppette with video rental and a ten-pump gas station. They walked past signs advertising Sunday brunch at the Officer's Club and bingo at the

NCO Club. They walked past the sweep of the chapel roof and through the maze of enlisted housing and into the officers' section. They walked past house after house, down the streets named after states . . . Alabama, Colorado, New Hampshire . . . and streets named after generals . . . Langley, Fairchild, Mitchell . . . and the streets named after aircraft . . . Falcon, Stratofortress, Phantom. . . .

"We could have waited five more minutes and ridden in your dad's car," said Gari.

"Didn't want to," said Bo.

Later that night, Bo asked Gari if he could have the trumpet mouthpiece back.

"Wipe it off when you're done," she said.

Bo silently played along to Taps in his room. In his head, he relived the finale to the Flying Farmer's act. The announcer, step by step, had talked the farmer out of the sky and down onto firm ground, complete with a staged bumpy landing and a wild careening ride down the taxiway. At the end, the farmer had stumbled from the plane, lifting his battered straw hat to the applauding crowd.

Bo put the trumpet mouthpiece down on the windowsill near his bed. He fell asleep and dreamed that he was the Flying Farmer, but his plane was streaming tape out the back instead of white smoke. He dove and flipped and rolled through the hallways of Young Oaks, holding his breath and looking and looking for the runway where his dad had said he was supposed to land.

Gari was awake during Taps too. She had gotten another e-mail from her mom.

I have to disagree with you about there being nothing to show me in North Carolina. There's beauty everywhere. Use your camera to find it.
I'm thinking of you — All the time,
Mom

Gari held her mom's old army figure tightly until the last sad note had played, and then she slipped it under her pillow. She didn't want to risk losing it again.

23
OUTSIDE THE TAPED SPACE

On Monday morning, Miss Loupe, wearing a plain black shirt, frowned at the notes the substitute teacher had left. She stood outside the Taped Space and spoke to her class.

"This is what Marc was wearing when they rescued him." She held up a round emblem with a bolt of lightning embroidered on it. "This patch saved his life."

"They found him?" said Aimee and Martina at the same time.

"Where is he, ma'am?" asked Melissa.

"Did you talk to him?" said Allison.

"How?" said Bo. "How did it save his life?"

"Can we see the patch?" said Rick.

"Was there a great battle?" said Trey.

"There *was* a great battle. But Marc's side didn't win," said Miss Loupe. "Six of his friends died."

She handed the patch to Rick in the front row, who held on to it for a moment, then passed it to Allison beside him. It slowly traveled throughout the class as Miss Loupe spoke.

"Marc ended up alone, hiding in a crevice — that's a kind of crack — deep in the mountains of Afghanistan. I don't think the rescue team would've found him because he had gotten too weak to cry out. The only reason they did was because he threw his patch out when they came near. But the patch was so small that at first the rescuers didn't see it."

A chorus of voices broke out: "But you said — then how did — where did you — ?"

"Because when it landed, the patch startled a bird. . . ." Miss Loupe's words began to break apart. ". . . It flew up . . . out of the crevice . . . squawking . . . and the team came . . . and they found him."

Melissa scribbled in her notebook. "What kind of bird, Miss Loupe?"

"Why is *that* important?" said Zac.

"I'm writing . . . Never mind." Melissa drew a little question mark in the margin of her notes.

Miss Loupe continued. "They called in a helicopter, and then they flew him on a larger plane to a hospital with a medical team, and —"

"My mom does that! That's what she does!" Gari spoke before she could stop herself. "In Iraq."

"Please thank your mother for me, then," said Miss Loupe. Her eyes stayed on Gari's face. "A team like hers saved Marc's life."

But Gari noticed that Miss Loupe was biting her lip. Hard. There was a raw spot on her bottom lip.

"He's not in Afghanistan anymore. They flew him to a base hospital in Germany, and then back to the States," continued Miss Loupe.

"He's fine?" Bo said. "He's going to be all right? Everything's okay?"

"No," said Miss Loupe. She looked sideways at the Taped Space, but she didn't step in. "I know you're used to me pretending all sorts of crazy things. But I'm not going to pretend now."

She watched as Trey handed the patch to Bo.

"Marc will never be the same. They had to amputate his left foot. He's blind in one eye."

"He won't be able to fight?" said Trey.

"Which eye did he lose?" said Melissa.

"Did you go see him?" said Bo. The underside of the patch was rough in his hands. The lightning bolt on it looked exactly like the sky was splitting.

"Yes," said Miss Loupe. "But he didn't recognize me."

At that moment, the fire alarm rang. And rang. And rang.

OO-GAH! OO-GAH! OO-GAH!

The students automatically got up from their desks and lined up at the door.

OO-GAH! OO-GAH!

Miss Loupe stayed frozen in her spot outside of the Taped Space.

OO-GAH! OO-GAH!

Her students had to come back and guide her out of the classroom.

24
EMERGENCY

Engine fire, left engine. Engine fire on the left.

That's all Gari could think as they marched outside. Every time her left foot hit the ground, dialogue from an old movie played in her head.

Engine fire, left. Engine fire, left.

It was a movie she and her mom had watched last November.

Begin the emergency procedure checklist!

Engine fire, left. Engine fire, left.

It was an Air Force movie, not an Army one.

It's not working! Nothing's working!

Engine fire, left. Engine fire, left.

Gari's mom had yelled at the TV:

"Don't just stand there, soldier, do something!"

Gari had laughed at her mom, talking Army to an Air Force pilot in an old plane on a little screen. But she suddenly knew how her mom had felt, watching and being unable to do anything.

Left! His left foot was gone.

25
ORDINARY THINGS

While they were outside, waiting for the fire alarm to be turned off, Rick asked Miss Loupe where her loupe (with a little l) was. Martina remembered seeing the cord break before Miss Loupe had run outside. Sanjay asked her to retrace her route, near the younger grades' rusty jungle gym. Bo explained how a FOD walk worked. Mr. Nix, whose class kept making dashes for the playground equipment instead of standing still in line, volunteered his students to help.

"One STRAIGHT line, first graders! PARALLEL to the line formed by the sixth grade."

Amazingly, the first graders formed an orderly line and marched with quiet intensity, inspecting every blade of grass. Tony found the loupe in less than five minutes.

"We have a GIANT card for you too. It's from Hawaii," he said as he handed the brass teardrop back to her. "You can look at it with your special eye."

Miss Loupe nodded slowly and thanked him. Her earrings didn't move or twinkle.

At lunch, the boys had to sit with the girls. No one said a word to one another, until Allison offered Rick half of an Oreo (the half without the creamy filling, but he took it). Then Martina started talking about the air show, and Bo used a milk carton to demonstrate how the Flying Farmer buzzed the crowd. Zac moved his chair over from the next table and said something about a girl being on the Thunderbird team now, and Shaunelle moved her chair too, and said yeah, she was good, and Aimee said she liked the demonstration of how the paratroopers jump in behind enemy lines. Then Trey drew a picture on his napkin of Marc's unit being attacked and everyone crowded around one table and passed it around.

"What if they hadn't found him?" said Zac.

"What do you think?" said Sanjay.

They cleaned up their tables as carefully as they could. Then they chose Allison and Rick to approach Mrs. Purdy for a favor.

The next day, the principal and the cafeteria manager carried the Ugly, Ugly Couch from the lunchroom back into Miss Loupe's classroom. As they tilted it through the doorway, the class could see all the signatures on the bottom, including Marc's.

"I need this *out* of my lunchroom," said Mrs. Purdy, looking at Miss Loupe with a faint smile.

"Until the School Commission makes up their mind about when to visit again," said Mrs. Heard. She sneezed.

Miss Loupe nodded again to say thanks. But she looked away from the couch after they left. Her black slippers stayed under her desk.

Later that week, during library time, Shaunelle looked up Miss Loupe's former boyfriend, Eric Browne, on the library's computer.

"Who's he?" asked Gari.

Martina explained about his name being under the couch. "Maybe they couldn't be together anymore after Miss Loupe came to Reform," she said. She leaned a tiny bit closer to Sanjay. He didn't move away.

"There's an Eric Browne in L.A. who buys old houses and fixes them up. Do you think that's him?" said Shaunelle. The mansion in the ad with Eric Browne's name was made of gray stone and had pointy turrets, like Miss Candy's drawings of her Reading Castle. The little sign that hung from a wooden post in the front yard said OPEN HOUSE.

"What's an open house?" Zac asked.

"It's when anyone can come in to look," translated Kylie. "My mom does them all the time."

"So?" said Allison. "Why are we looking at this dumb house?"

"I was hoping he'd be . . . a multimillionaire," said Shaunelle. "Like in books. Where someone who is long lost turns out to be worth oodles of money."

"Why do we need money?" Sanjay spoke up. "Miss Loupe doesn't need money. She needs . . . I don't know. She needs . . ."

No one could finish his sentence.

When they returned to Room 208 from the library, Miss Loupe let them all have free reading time. She sat at her desk and opened her own book, but she didn't turn the pages.

Behind the cover of his library book, Bo took a pen and began to cover the back of his hand with tiny black dots. Sometimes, when his dad flew hard and fast, the force of pulling against gravity broke blood vessels in his legs. He had shown Bo the purple speckles on his calves and feet, which the pilots called G-measles. You couldn't see gravity, but you could see what it did to you.

Miss Loupe could make them see things that weren't there too. She could make you believe that a couch was worth talking to, that cracks were infinitely important, and that anything that happened between four lines of slightly dingy masking tape was as real as a scar on your leg. Bo looked over his book at Miss Loupe, who was staring over his head at the wall behind him. You couldn't see Miss Loupe's sadness, but you could see what it was doing to her.

Four rows to his left, Gari sat at Dillon's old desk, with the book club selection propped up in front of her. She wasn't reading.

She wished her Plan B had actually happened. She wished she hadn't believed her mom when she'd said her assignment wasn't dangerous. The box of donated toys and school supplies for Marc was still sitting in front of Miss Loupe's desk, its cardboard flaps sticking out like wings. The School Commission wasn't coming back any time soon. She'd have to come up with a new plan. Before it was too late.

Miss Loupe kept looking at the clock hands as they clicked forward inside their bent cage, every five minutes for the rest of the day.

26
DO SOMETHING

Two weeks went by. Two weeks of Gari waking up to Reveille and listening to Taps play at night. Two weeks of walking to school, past a gate guard, instead of being driven by her mom. Two weeks of sharing a bathroom with Bo, who left toothpaste blobs on the faucets. Two weeks of being still in elementary at Young Oaks and not in middle school at SeaJA. Two weeks of watching Miss Loupe read out loud from the textbook and avoid the Taped Space. Two weeks of waiting and waiting and waiting for her mom to call, and when she finally did, getting cut off in midsentence by the operator. Two weeks in which Gari planned what to do next.

Finally, one day, when the last bell rang, releasing the Young Oaks students to walk home, Gari headed straight for the bathroom on the kindergarten hall. No one had discovered her work. No one had gone in because of the sign and the terrible smell. No one had seen her art at all.

Last night, she had found a large manila envelope on Uncle Phil's desk. She had written a note headlined BRING THEM HOME NOW, signed her full name to it, and slipped it in. She had carefully addressed the envelope to the local paper: *The*

Reform Chronicle, Reform, North Carolina, Attn: News Department. All she had to do now was take pictures of the damage she had done, get them developed, and mail them off.

When the story showed up on the front page of the paper, she would be in big trouble. The Air Force and the Army couldn't ignore such an action, not when she was the niece of the base commander, could they? They would make her clean up the mess, yes, but after seeing her pictures, they couldn't hide what had happened. Her mom would see that Gari didn't belong in this place, that she would have to come home and make a new plan. She would never lose an eye. Or a foot. They would both return to Seattle. And Gari would go to Seattle Junior Academy, where nobody — *nobody* — had a parent doing anything dumb.

She knelt down on the bathroom floor and took a picture of the line of little green figures she'd glued to the sink. She stood up and framed a shot of the writing on the mirror. She turned her lens to the overflowing pools of red on the floor.

But she couldn't shake the feeling that something was wrong with her plan.

What if Miss Loupe thought she was insulting Marc somehow . . . what if this wasn't the right moment to . . .

It is! It is! she told herself as she snapped more pictures. *You're ready. Everything's ready. Nothing is wrong.*

When she was finished, she hid the camera in her backpack and escaped from the stench of the enclosed room. The halls had emptied quickly and were now silent and dark, like a tunnel. She ran to the front door, but near the map on the wall, she stopped.

Her stars!

They were still in her desk. Hundreds of them.

They're paper. Paper. That's all. I can leave them and get them tomorrow.

But each star had been folded while thinking about her mom. They had already stolen them from her once. If she got them, maybe she would get rid of this snaking doubt that was creeping through her brilliant plan. She was already dreading waiting through even more days until her pictures were developed.

She raced toward Room 208.

When she reached it, she stopped dead. The lights were on.

She peered inside the small window on the door.

Bo, Melissa, and Trey were inside the Taped Space. Melissa had her notebook. Trey was sketching something on the back of what looked like the Student Handbook. Bo was pacing up one side of the taped rectangle and down the other, over and over. He looked up and saw her.

Bo opened the door and grabbed her arm. "Get in here! Somebody will see you!"

"What are you talking about? I just want my —"

He dragged her into the room and into the Taped Space. Gari looked at Melissa, Bo, and Trey.

"We need you," Bo said. "What are we going to do about Miss Loupe?"

27

WHICH BATTLE ARE YOU IN?

"We're not supposed to be in a classroom after the bell," said Melissa. "Mrs. Heard is going to find us and kick us out."

"No," said Bo. "We're staying. We need the Taped Space. Something is broken, because Miss Loupe hasn't stepped in here since Marc was hurt."

"Yeah," said Trey. "Not once. She's so . . . so . . . blank."

Melissa hurried to the light switch and turned it off. She peeked through the door window into the hallway, then turned around and said in a loud whisper to Trey, "Wouldn't you be blank if your brother was in a hospital?"

"But she said Marc was getting better. She said he knew he was in the States now and not still in Afghanistan. She said they were going to fix his foot. If he's getting better, then how come she's not?"

"We have to fix gravity," said Bo.

"What?" said Gari.

"You can't see gravity, but it's important," insisted Bo. "The same for whatever's in this Taped Space. It's important to Miss Loupe. Tell her, Melissa. Read her what's in your notebook."

The four of them stood inside the boundaries of the tape. Melissa scanned her notebook for the right page. She read Miss Loupe's words:

"What happens when we place an object in the Taped Space? Do we see it differently than if it were in the teachers' lounge or in a living room?"

"Why, indeed? Why are some systems closed and some are open?"

"I guess I'll have to put on my shark-proof diving suit. . . ."

"Earlier than that!" said Bo.

Melissa flipped back several pages.

"Art needs a — "

Trey jumped in: "Frame. Art needs a frame! We need the Taped Space because it's a *frame*."

Gari threw her backpack off her shoulders and banged it into the Taped Space. "Woo-hoo! I put my backpack in the frame and now it's art. NO. Art takes work. It takes planning. It takes —" She broke off. "Forget it."

"Let me see your army man," said Bo. He grabbed on to her backpack.

"Hey!" Gari tried to drag her backpack away from him. What if he found her envelope? Or her camera?

"You said it wasn't a toy; it was art!"

Gari said nothing but held on to the strap of her bag tightly.

"I gave it back to you once, didn't I?" said Bo.

"Yes, but — " Maybe if she let him see it, he would leave her backpack alone. She cautiously took the little green figure out of her pocket. Bo put the army man into the Taped Space and stared at it.

"We have one object," he said. "Now we need something else."

"You're making this all up as you go along!" said Gari.

"What's wrong with making things up?"

"Everything," said Gari. "If you want to help Miss Loupe and her brother, you have to have a plan."

Melissa was folding a corner of her notebook cover back and forth and watching the door. "I think we should get some teachers or Miss Candy to help us."

Bo jumped up and began to pace inside the Taped Space.

"New Recruit, what about you?" he said to the army man. "Quit staring at your toes and pay attention! Do you know where you are? Or have you never even looked?"

Trey laughed. Melissa opened her mouth, then closed it and quickly wrote something down in her notebook. She held her pencil at the ready.

Gari stared at Bo. Had he lost his mind?

Bo warmed up to his role. "Come on, New Recruit! Move your feet! Move it! Move it! Move it!" he barked.

Melissa's pencil flew over the page. "Oh, that's perfect!"

"Perfect for what?" said Trey. He tried to twist her notebook away so he could see what she was writing.

Melissa pulled the notebook back and aimed her pencil at him, point-first. "A play! I'm already writing one, and Miss Loupe can direct it, and Bo could be in it, and —"

"What good would that do?" Gari broke in. "Besides, I think Miss Loupe's going to get fired."

"What?" Melissa almost dropped her pencil. "She can't get fired. How do you know?"

"Well, maybe she'll quit before they can fire her," said Gari. "Because right now, she can't even handle a fire drill. I don't think they'll let her keep being a teacher."

They all turned on her. She put her fists on her hips. "Well, it's true!"

Why couldn't they see that everything was falling apart?

"There they all were," said Trey. He walked over to the chalkboard and drew a picture of the school, with an amoebalike presence around it. "Deep in the Quagmire of Ignorance. They were up to their necks. They had quicksand tickling their throats. . . ." He began to add little green figures around the perimeter of the school, reaching in to save the sinking students.

Melissa looked at the arms reaching in to rescue the disappearing bodies. She flipped to another page in her notebook. "'Be kind.' That's what she said to do: Be kind."

I'm walking out. I still have my pictures. I still have my plan. This is —

Gari stopped when she saw what Trey was now drawing: a battlefield, except this one was set in the interior of the school. It was a map of the hallways, the cafeteria, the principal's office, the library, and the classrooms. He filled them all with soldiers, holding their positions, ready to fight.

It was like her Plan B, except bigger and better.

Bo was showing Trey's drawing to the little green figure.

"You see, soldier," he barked in his drill sergeant's voice, "art is arranging objects — even you! — to create BEAUTY."

.Gari felt like stars were exploding inside her.

That's what was wrong with her plan. Yeah, it might bring her mom home. It might get her out of here. But what picture would it leave in her mom's head of *her*?

Her plan didn't create anything beautiful. And her mom would know it. All the time.

There was a noise in the hall. Footsteps. Melissa gasped.

Gari grabbed her backpack and the little green man and ran to the window. She lifted the frame and crawled out. Bo was right behind her. Melissa. Trey. One by one, they flipped themselves over the sill and thumped onto the grass. Trey reached up and slid the windowpane back down. They crouched in the patchy grass underneath and pressed their backs against the rough brick wall.

Any minute now, someone was going to see them. Any. Minute. Now.

They saw a light come on in the classroom. They heard the muffled sound of the trash can being emptied. The bang of a mop against a pail.

Gari gripped the lone battered army figure in her fist.

Pick your battles, baby. Pick your battles, or you'll lose them all.

"Come on," said Gari.

In single file, they hugged the side of the building and followed her around to the other side of the school.

"Where are we going? We should just go home!" said Melissa.

"I'm not sure which one it is," said Gari. She surveyed the windows. She thought she was in the right place, but she might be lost. One window was smaller than the rest, dark and cramped.

She peered inside. Yes.

Her mom helped save wounded soldiers. She knew how to help save Miss Loupe.

"Look."

Bo stuck his face near the glass.

"I can't see anything. It's too dark."

"Wait."

I'm sorry, Mom. If I do this, you'll have to stay over there a while. And I'll have to stay here.

Bo's eyes adjusted. It was a bathroom. In the dank and shadowed space, he saw piles of little green figures lying all over the sinks and the floors.

"Wow! Did you do that?"

Melissa looked. Then Trey.

Gari took a deep breath.

"We have to change what Miss Loupe is *seeing*," she said. "We have to make it beautiful."

"How do you know what Miss Loupe is seeing?" said Melissa. "How can you be sure?"

Gari said slowly, "Because that..." She gestured at the window. "That's what's in my head too."

The flight suit in the glass case flashed into Bo's mind. He knew exactly what Gari meant.

"I think we should post soldiers like those all over the school," said Gari. "But not lying down. Upright. Thousands of them."

"Why?" said Trey.

"Because," said Bo. He looked directly at Gari. "Everyone you know is fighting a great battle."

Gari nodded.

Bo continued, "And we're in this one with Miss Loupe."

Maybe it was the Taped Space still holding them together. Maybe it was like a camera lens had framed the four of them, and someone snapped a picture they could all be part of. Or maybe it was that they each thought, for a split second, where they would be standing in the school if someone came to them and said what Mrs. Heard had said to Miss Loupe. They didn't see how the whole thing would play out, not yet, but...

"Yes," said Trey.

"Yes," said Melissa.

"Yes," said Bo.

"The first thing to do," said Gari, "is get those men out of that bathroom. I don't want *that* to be what anyone sees first."

"We'll go in and get them," said Bo.

"I Super Glued them to the floor," said Gari.

"No problem," said Bo.

Gari's bruise above her eye started to ache. "YES, it's a problem! I can't —"

"I mean, no problem getting off Super Glue. I accidentally glued some pennies to the inside of the dryer once."

"Accidentally?" said Melissa.

Bo shrugged. "Mom used nail polish remover and they came right off."

"Mrs. Purdy has nail polish," said Melissa. "I bet she has remover too."

"I'll go," said Trey. He punched Bo's arm and grinned. "You can't afford to get caught, weenie. Your dad would KILL you."

Bo punched back. "Yours wouldn't?"

But he thought, *Dad? This is the right thing, isn't it?*

They met again the next day. And the next. Each day that week, they left the school by the front door, and each day, they came back in by the window. They sat in the Taped Space with the army figures they had rescued and made their plans.

Gari proposed that they break down, step by step, how they would accomplish their goal. "It's going to take longer than you think to fill a whole school," she warned.

"Yes, and we should get other people to help too," said Melissa. "We should start with Miss Candy. Everybody goes into the library."

"Yes, and we need a BIG reason for them to help us," said Bo. "Not just for art. For a good cause. My mom does scholarships and stuff. She gets people to say *yes* all the time."

Trey said, "Yes, and we should draw or take pictures of everything. Pictures make people pay attention. And . . . uh . . . Mrs. Heard likes them."

Bo took all the little green figures out of Gari's bag and arranged and rearranged them while he listened. Finally, he jumped up and started pacing, addressing the room:

"Got it, New Recruits? We started at the beginning, and we're fighting our way to the end. In case you forget, I'm right here to kick your butt!"

"Knock it off, Bo," said Gari. "First things first."

Bo picked up one of the little green figures and tucked it into position on Miss Loupe's desk.

"This one *is* first," he said. "Go ahead. Take the picture."

Gari zeroed in on the soldier and snapped the first picture on her new roll of film. The four of them left Room 208 and quietly closed the window.

The next day, Miss Loupe found a single green figure next to Marc's framed quote. And a note:

**I don't know, but I'm told it's true,
You're not lost till they stop looking for you.**

It was the start of Operation Yes.

PLAN

C

28
EVERYONE SAID YES, BUT . . .

The second little green man (or LGM, as Melissa named them) appeared in Miss Candy's butterscotch candies dish. The easy part was placing it there, because Miss Candy was always away from her desk, helping someone find a book. The hard part was photographing it without anyone noticing. Luckily, when the School Commission announced that they couldn't revisit Young Oaks for at least three months because of "prior commitments," Mrs. Heard had allowed work on the Reading Castle to resume. The loud whirr and click of the camera was lost in the buzz of Miss Candy's rotary saw.

"Maybe you've got a secret Army boyfriend," Airman Kresge said with a grin when Miss Candy found the soldier. "Maybe I'll have to go beat him up."

Miss Candy rolled her eyes. She put the LGM front and center on her desk and waited to see what would happen next.

Gari had a harder time with the third LGM, because Trey deployed it in a tree overlooking the playground.

"He's guarding the perimeter," insisted Trey. Gari made him hoist her up on his back so she could take the picture.

"*Inside* from now on," she said. She hoped having human supporters would not make a mess of her plans.

In the cafeteria, Mrs. Purdy knew something was up when some of the boys still wanted to sit with the girls, even after she'd removed the tape and told them that if they behaved, they could return to their former seats. She was especially observant on the day when Bo and Gari and Melissa and Trey took turns whispering to the rest of the class huddled around them. If they were talking to one another, then they probably weren't planning another food fight. She was pleased that her seat assignments had worked.

So when Bo came to her and asked to place an army figure to guard the crack in her cash register, she played along. When Gari aimed the camera in her direction, she smiled and patted her curls. But she had a strong feeling that she was not the focus of the picture.

Once the rest of the class was in on the plan, LGM began to appear more rapidly around the school.

Zac left several next to the lost and found box in the school office. Kylie posted hers on top of the EXIT sign next to the map in the front hallway. Martina put an LGM in the girls' bathroom, but it was okay because it was actually an LGW. She was on duty over the yellowed porcelain sink, the one with no plug in the drain, which was dangerous because anything, even she, could fall down it.

Allison decided to approach Mr. Nix through her little brother, Tony. She gave him a bag of LGM to take to his class, along with a fake sixth-grade worksheet on estimating group sizes, on which she'd circled several wrong answers and written: "You should already know this! This is first-grade material!" By the day's end, twenty LGM were lined up in a neat row along the top ledge of Mr. Nix's chalkboard. He added and removed a number of them each morning, to see if his class could tell instantly if there were more or less than the day before.

Day after day, more and more LGM appeared at strategic spots around the school, until they had used every one of the rescued soldiers they had started with. Gari had a stack of developed pictures, and Trey had a map of where each figure was placed, and Melissa had a notebook filled with their plans for the future. Bo had so much energy built up inside him that he ran to school without stopping.

It was time to go public with their plan. But first, they wanted to tell Miss Loupe.

She had noticed the LGM and the new quote they'd left on her desk, of course.

"There are more?" she said. "In the school? Why didn't I notice?"

Melissa started to tell her that she'd worn the same shirt three days in a row this week, so it wasn't surprising that . . . But, no. Better not to point out that detail.

They didn't reveal all of the plan, not yet. But Trey showed her the map. "Here they are. So far."

Gari showed her each picture. Miss Loupe studied the one of the LGM in the tree.

Bo cut to the chase. "Will Marc like it?" Miss Loupe had said Marc could talk to her on the phone for a few minutes now. And that he was getting used to his artificial foot. But did he remember Room 208?

Miss Loupe agreed. He would like it.

"Are you sure you want to take on a project this big?" she said. "I mean, I love it, and you're wonderful to help him, but —"

"Trust us," said Bo. "It's going to be great."

They brought Melissa's notebook, Trey's drawing, and Gari's developed pictures to Mrs. Heard's office. Bo presented her with an LGM and asked, with his best grin, if she would pose with it beside the rusty bear mascot in front of the school.

"For the paper," he said. "We want a reporter to come to Young Oaks."

The principal was astonished at what had been happening right under her nose, but she liked the idea of a reporter coming to the school. After she had her picture taken, she placed the LGM by her phone. It made a satisfying clicking noise when she tapped it against her desk while calling the School Commission.

"Yes. Yes. A reporter *will* be here, looking around. Just letting you know."

Before the story appeared in the paper, Bo asked his dad if he could ride along in the official car.

"Can I drive?" he said as he hopped in.

"No," said his dad.

"Can I have some of your coffee?"

"Try it," said his dad. "You won't like it."

"Can I tell you about a secret plan?"

"Yes," said his dad. "Is this briefing classified?"

The article in the *Reform Chronicle* was published with this headline:

STUDENTS AT YOUNG OAKS PLAN TO DEPLOY 100,000 TROOPS

In the article, the reporter admitted to fudging the numbers for the air show attendance.

"You see," she wrote, "when I described the crowd last month, I used the words 'up to 30,000,' because that covers everything from one person to thousands. But the students at Young Oaks want to be more precise. They are counting.

"They want to collect and deploy throughout their school exactly 100,000 little plastic army figures — each purchased for a donation of one dollar. When they have reached their goal, they will celebrate by giving the entire amount to the care of wounded soldiers."

Bo was quoted in the article as saying: "When you see a problem, you can't lie there with your tongue sticking out, playing dead."

Gari was quoted as saying: "War. There should be a better plan."

At the end of the article, Melissa was quoted as saying: "Be kind. And take good notes." The reporter thought that was brilliant, and she admired Melissa's well-organized, nearly full, color-coded notebook. She also told Gari that digital cameras were much more practical and loaned her one for the project. "This one will take up to two thousand pictures at a time," she said.

Miss Loupe posted the newspaper story in her classroom. She sent copies to her sister in Japan, to her younger brother at the Air Force Academy, and to her mom and dad.

Please read this to Marc, she wrote above the headline.

After they read it, her mom and dad taped the article to the wall in Marc's room at Walter Reed Army Medical Center.

Gari printed out the e-mail her mom had sent and brought it in to the class too.

My FOB tour was short but amazing. I got to fly in a helicopter! But more importantly, I learned what happens to my patients as soon as they are brought in from the battlefield, and how they are prepped for the helicopter ride to our hospital. Just like you said happened with your teacher's brother, Marc.

It's different being here than working in home health care, but I'm learning something new every day. I hope you are too.

XOXO from my medical team. They will be sending a donation soon. What the class is planning to do is beautiful.

All the time,

Mom

P.S. Don't forget to send that reporter a thank-you note!

After the article appeared, Sanjay suggested they invite the whole town to see what they were doing. "We'll make it an open house!" he said. They didn't tell Miss Loupe, but he and Martina also sent a copy of the paper to her old boyfriend Eric Browne. They circled the real-estate ads for properties that needed renovating in Reform.

For the open house, the Base Exchange store placed a special order from the factory for a large shipment of LGM. Mrs. Heard helped the class set up a separate bank account for the donations, and, with her approval, a container of LGM was placed in the front hallway, under the map. Mrs. Heard spent one weekend repainting the coastlines and redrawing the meandering path of the Mississippi River, as well as re-bluing both oceans. She added a special star near Washington, D.C., not just because it was the nation's capital, but because Walter Reed Medical Center was there, and inside the rehabilitation wing, Marc was waging his great battle.

Most of Reform came to Young Oaks on open house night, including the mayor. He purchased fifty LGM and had his picture taken with Room 208 outside the school in front of the yellow-ribboned oaks.

Gari asked him if he was running for reelection.

"You're always running," he said. "You never stop."

"Even in a small place like Reform?"

"Especially here."

Miss Loupe stationed herself in Room 208 and greeted visitors as they came in. She showed them Marc's picture and told them the story of his rescue. She met Colonel Whaley for the first time.

"Bo tells me you used to live on base," he said.

"Yes, on Colorado Street," she replied. "My dad was an instructor pilot."

"And now you're an instructor too," he said.

He walked around the Ugly, Ugly Couch and looked down at the Taped Space. He read all the posters on the walls. He touched Bo's name on the list of the Ugly Couch Players.

"I see why Bo likes school for the first time in his life," he said.

After he left, Miss Loupe allowed herself a small smile.

For each LGM purchased, Melissa recorded the donation in a separate notebook, and Trey showed the sponsor where on his school diagram it could be placed. Gari insisted on this.

"It can't be random! We're *arranging* them, not playing with them!"

Melissa agreed. She liked the way Gari's plan was emerging, and she liked the shape of the play forming in her notebook. They would take that part of Operation Yes to Miss Loupe soon enough.

Melissa also liked the way she and Gari had started walking around the perimeter of the playground together after lunch.

"Do you think Rick smells good?" she said.

"Sometimes," said Gari.

"He says he's going to pierce his ear next year."

"Cool. Very West Coast."

"Bo's cute too."

"Ugh," said Gari.

*　　*　　*

Miss Candy's half-built Reading Castle was a popular spot for the LGM. Airman Kresge used his day off to help her finish more walls. Mrs. Purdy's lunch line was also a favorite location. She washed each LGM before placing it on top of a section of her gleaming, stainless-steel service shelves. Mrs. Heard let her office filing cabinets be covered with as many as would fit. She even purchased the handful that were still in her desk drawer and deployed them along the sills of her tiny windows.

Some of the LGM didn't stay at the school. They traveled around with the persons that had bought them. This was okay, Room 208 agreed, as long as they were returned for the night of the show.

Bo kept at least three men in his pockets, and he was always pulling them out and rearranging them into scenes on his desktop, or beside his lunch tray, or even along the back of the Ugly, Ugly Couch. His mom took one to work with her, in the pocket of her athletic shorts. His dad zipped one, along with his loose change, into his flight suit pocket each day when he got dressed for work.

Melissa had only one, but she kept it clean, scrubbing the small triangle where the bent arm met the fixed leg with an old toothbrush, and rubbing a drop of Vaseline on the helmet to keep it shiny.

Shaunelle's littlest sister kept getting hold of hers, leaving teeth marks in its back, so she hid it behind her books while she was at school.

Trey had six or seven, which took on real faces when he sketched them, with scars and grimaces and bloody wounds. He drew them in helicopters and in hospital beds. He drew them throwing themselves on top of grenades and standing guard at the Tomb of the Unknown Soldier. He drew them without legs and without fear.

Operation Yes seemed to be going well. Young Oaks was behind it, and the town of Reform too. But . . .

Over the winter break, Miss Loupe drove to Washington, D.C., to see Marc. She brought back a picture of the two of them in Santa hats. Marc had a patch over one eye. In the background, Bo could see the GET WELL poster they'd all signed and sent. Dozens of Gari's pictures of LGM covered the wall. Several of the nurses and staff at Walter Reed had sent donations.

"Is he doing better?" asked Gari.

"It's slow," said Miss Loupe. She tucked the picture of her and Marc next to the framed quote and the little green man guarding it. "We didn't expect his recovery to take this long."

"Did you see your dad?" asked Bo.

Miss Loupe nodded. "He asked about all of you."

She stopped reading them the lessons out of the textbook and began to teach them science and math and social studies and language arts with more enthusiasm. But when they asked about the Ugly Couch Players and theater camp next summer, she didn't tell them that she was thinking of not coming back. And she didn't mention that she had done nothing further with her grant proposal. The Taped Space was there, waiting, but Miss Loupe never stepped in.

By the end of January, Room 208 had collected only 4,092 LGM. A long way from 100,000.

29
A LONG WAY FROM 100,000

Before school, Bo, Trey, Gari, and Melissa met beside the rusty jungle gym on the little kids' playground. Around them, the trees were stripped of leaves, and the sky was as gray as the faded, smooth wood of the three old seesaws. A swing moved slightly in the cold wind, creaking on its chains.

"Why did you tell that reporter we could get one hundred thousand dollars?" said Bo. "Don't you know how many zeros that is?"

Melissa pursed her lips. "I didn't pick that number. We ALL did."

"One hundred thousand is not that much," said Gari. "If we were in Seattle, we would be there already."

"Earth to Gari," said Bo. "You don't live in Seattle anymore."

"Maybe we should change our goal," said Trey.

"To what?" said Gari.

"Maybe we should change who's running this operation," said Bo. "You and Melissa keep walking around and around after lunch, and you never say what you're talking about!"

Melissa's neck flushed a deep red. She zipped her jacket up to her chin.

Gari bumped Bo's arm. "We can talk about whatever we want. You aren't the boss of us."

Trey held up his drawing of the school, which was filled with tiny X's where LGM had been placed. There were large white spaces with number goals written next to them. "The problem is that it isn't big enough," he said.

"Everyone's working hard," insisted Melissa.

Trey shook his head. "I mean the circumference. We haven't drawn a big enough circle of people. We have to think about who's outside who could be on the *inside*."

"Yes," said Gari. "To increase our probability of being heard."

"Right," said Melissa, thinking of Miss Loupe's ball as it had bounced around Room 208. "We should think of people we have things in common with, people who aren't in the circle now, but who could be."

"Other schools?"

"People who used to be in the military?"

"The Flying Farmer!"

"What?"

"He used to be in the military. Think of all the people who see his show," said Bo.

"It's a start," said Gari. "We'll make a list of everybody and everything and plan how to reach them. Make the circle bigger and bigger and bigger."

Gari was right, but Bo was starting to think that even a circle a million miles wide wouldn't get Miss Loupe back into the Taped Space.

"I don't think we should wait," he said. "We should start rehearsing the show now."

"I haven't finished writing it!" said Melissa.

"We'll make it up as we go along," said Bo. "We have to."

"But we planned for the LGM to be part of the show," said Gari. "Isn't that in your script, Melissa? What if we don't have enough? What if it looks silly? What if people won't come? What if . . ."

A pair of jets flew overhead, drowning out her words. The four of them looked up, watching the streaks of white trail across the gray sky.

They flew so straight, thought Bo. They had a mission, a plan, and a flight path. He didn't know how to move ahead that way. He was always up and down and around and around, like a pogo stick.

"What if Miss Loupe doesn't come back next year?" he said.

"*You* won't be back," Trey pointed out. Bo still hadn't told him he might be staying. There was no official word on his dad's assignment.

"The reason she came here was because she loved theater. I don't think she does anymore. She thinks it doesn't matter. She thinks we can't see that she's all cracked. But we can." He hoped they could follow his jumps. "We have to get Miss Loupe to take off again, even if it's bumpy."

"You want to goof off instead of working on my plan," said Gari.

"You're afraid that if you get on stage, you'll stink!"

"I'm not doing acting!"

"Yes, you are. We're going to do the play, and you're going to be the New Recruit. I'm going to teach you, and you are going to be as BAD as possible."

Gari *was* bad. Worse even than Bo thought she could be.

"You're supposed to *look* clueless and bumbly, not actually *be* clueless and bumbly," he said. "Like the Flying Farmer, you know?"

"I didn't see the Flaming Farmer," said Gari. "Remember?"

"I'll show you."

Bo asked his mom to back the cars out of the garage. He taped a rectangle to the floor.

"Pretend this is the airspace above show center," he said. "Everything has to stay within the box or the audience can't see it."

He threw out his arms and buzzed into the space. He staggered from side to side, turning and dipping and barely catching himself inches above the floor. He ended by demonstrating a one-wheeled landing, sliding on his pant leg to a precise stop at the edge.

"But I'm not going to be an airplane. I'm supposed to be a person," objected Gari. "Didn't you read the script?"

"Yes, and the script says that I talk and you don't! You're the New Recruit! You're scared and you're not sure where you are and you don't speak a single word! So you have to show all that in how you *move*."

"I thought that it would be easier."

"It would be . . . if you'd loosen up!" He dragged her into the Taped Space. "Now, fly!"

Gari weakly held out her arms and flapped them like a duck.

Bo wanted to take his dad's golf club and pretend to shoot her down.

"How about if we pogo stick instead?"

Gari shook her head.

"Jump rope?"

"No."

Bo's eyes lit on Indy's travel crate. Minutes later, he and Gari and Indy were in the backyard. The grass was winter brown and touched by only a hint of the sun as it lowered. They hadn't grabbed jackets, and the air chilled their arms.

"Take off your shoe," he said.

"It's cold!"

"Take it off!" said Bo. "You want me to help you or not?"

"Not," said Gari. "Let's *not* do the show. Or get someone else to play the New Recruit!"

Indy snuggled up next to her leg and laid her head against it. She looked up at Gari with adoring eyes. She gave a questioning whine.

"Fine. Take my shoe."

"And your sock."

Gari handed them over. Her foot was freezing in the stiff short grass.

"Indy, sit," Bo said. She sat.

"Indy, catch," he said. He threw Gari's sock into the air. Indy caught it. And ran.

"You . . . you . . ." Gari was torn between kicking him with the shoe she still had on and taking it off so she could throw both of them at his head. He sped up the stairs to the deck and stood watching her. She gave up and ran after Indy.

Indy dodged and jinked and leaped. She twisted and barrel-rolled and slid. Slobber coated Gari's sock and hunks of dead grass and reddish dirt too. Gari charged in Indy's wake, calling her name and flailing her arms to catch her. It was impossible. No matter how fast she was, Indy was several hairs faster.

Gari finally collapsed in defeat, sweat staining the front and the back of her shirt. She lay there, looking up at the sky, her side aching and her breath puffing into the cold air in jags so hard they hurt. Indy trotted over and dropped the filthy wad of wet sock on her chest.

"Bravo!" said Bo, calling down.

He was clapping and whistling. Indy licked Gari's face. Gari clutched the sock and closed her eyes.

"NOW you're ready to fall," said Bo.

Gari shook her head. He was insane.

"But you're loose," said Bo. He came off the deck and stood beside her. "Come on, get up! I'll show you." He pulled her to her feet and made a fist in front of the lower part of his stomach. "It all comes from your core. If you're strong there, it's easy."

He had Gari make a fist in front of her stomach.

"Everything else is relaxed," he said. "Don't worry; the grass is a guaranteed soft landing."

"It hurt before," said Gari.

"I'll fall with you. It'll be a *controlled* landing." He took her arm and the two of them crashed to the grass. Bo fell lightly, Gari with a louder thud on top of him.

"That didn't hurt," she said.

Bo twisted his body out from under her. His ear stung where she had jabbed an elbow into it. "Next time you're solo."

He backed away and motioned for her to get up. "Close your eyes and I'll make the sound for you to follow."

Gari shut her eyes. "SWOOOOOOOSH!" said Bo. Gari crumpled and hit before he had finished.

"Again!"

"SWOOOOOOSH!" Thud.

"No," said Bo. "Think of a note hanging in the air. A plane about to land. A pogo . . ."

But Gari suddenly thought of the sound a straw made sucking a drink to the bottom. She waved away Bo's words.

"SWOOOOOOOSH!" This time Gari imagined she was a tall glass being drained of soda, and she almost matched the length of his sound with the arc of her fall. It was strange to fall on purpose. To plan to let go. She didn't dissolve like a paper star drifting down to the liquid at the bottom of a cup. Instead, she felt powerful and weightless, both at once.

"That was *too* good," said Bo. "You've got to look at least a little clumsy. You're the New Recruit, remember?"

And so it went. The more clumsy and bumbly she was in the yard, and later in the Taped Space, the better Bo told her that she had done. They planned how to make her even more terrible the next time they rehearsed.

Meanwhile, they all worked on making the circle bigger.

Bo sent a copy of the newspaper article and a note to the Flying Farmer:

I've never gotten to meet you, but I think you are the greatest pilot ever. Do you think you could tell everyone at your air shows about our flight plan?

Signed,

Your biggest fan

Gari sent pictures of the LGM to Tandi at Seattle Junior Academy.

"We could be sister schools," she told Tandi on the phone. "You help us with this, and we'll help you with . . ." She wasn't sure. What would be big at SeaJA this year?

The secretary at SeaJA listened when Tandi told the principal about the project. She sent a donation along with a note saying she would put the photos in Gari's application file for next year.

"Why do you want to go to SeaJA anyway?" Bo asked Gari when the donation arrived. "Is it better than here?"

Instead of answering, she asked him a question:

"Did you ever get elected to anything? Did anybody ever vote for you?"

"Yup," said Bo. "One time I won an election on my third day at a brand-new school."

"Oh, like for class clown?"

"Second-grade class representative. Cool, huh?"

"But how? How did you get anyone to vote for you when they didn't even know your name?"

"Easy. I told them that I was the new kid. That I didn't have any friends *or* enemies. I told them that I would be the fairest, most representative-est class representative they'd ever had."

"That's all it took?"

"Uh, that, and I showed them my cool scar. You know, the one you gave me?"

Gari e-mailed herself some new goals for next year at SeaJA. "Plan C," she titled it. Or was it Plan D? She was losing track of all the ways she'd arranged and rearranged her big ideas this year.

"Come on," said Bo. "Time to rehearse. Let's practice your entrance."

Gari fell down at least fifteen times before Bo said she had it almost right.

Allison asked her grandfather, who really had been a POW, to send a message to all the veterans' organizations in the country. They put the word out in their newsletters and meetings. The actor who had played her grandfather in the TV movie sent a generous donation and a signed picture for Allison. She posted it outside Room 208's door so everyone could see it.

* * *

Kylie and Shaunelle went to local restaurants and businesses, asking for their support. Then the two of them thought of something even better. They asked Miss Candy for help in building a Web site for Operation Yes.

"We want it to be bigger than the local phone book," said Shaunelle.

"Way bigger than an open house," said Kylie.

Miss Candy helped them scan in Trey's map and upload several pictures of the LGM.

"We can't fit all of the pictures," said Shaunelle. "Not if we get one hundred thousand."

"I like these two," said Miss Candy. "The minesweeper and the binoculars guy — they look like they're searching for something, like we do in the library."

"How about if we feature one new LGM each day?" said Kylie. "And then have a page that we put all the donors' names on?"

"We should get Marc to write the story of his rescue. . . ."

". . . Yes, and use that picture of Miss Loupe and him together. . . ."

". . . And make sure we have the address of the school on there. . . ."

"Information about Walter Reed," said Shaunelle.

"A way to donate online," said Kylie. "Can we do that?"

In February, Trey's dad left with his unit for their scheduled four-month rotation to Afghanistan. Trey gave him lots and lots of drawings of LGM to pass around to everyone at his deployed base. One made its way to the *Stars and Stripes* newspaper, which wrote a story about Operation Yes. The paper went out to over 350,000 readers in military families stationed overseas.

$100,000 IS NO MILK RUN FOR THESE YOUNG STUDENTS! the headline read. It told the story of Marc, and Room 208, and their quest for 100,000 LGM, with one of Trey's drawings as an illustration. At the end was the address of the Web site at Young Oaks where readers could make donations.

Mrs. Purdy put that story up on her cash register.

"A milk run is a *routine* mission," said Mr. Nix to his class as they came through the line. "Does anyone know what the opposite of *routine* is?"

One of his first graders tried to raise her hand and dropped her pudding. A glob of it landed on his shoe.

"No, that's not it," said Mr. Nix.

But that week, Miss Candy called him for help to log over three hundred new donations through Shaunelle and Kylie's Web site.

A TV reporter from Raleigh saw the *Stars and Stripes* story online and phoned Colonel Whaley.

"The maintenance sergeant's son is your son's best friend? Your niece is masterminding the project. . . . Her mom — your sister — is deployed and . . . The wounded soldier's sister is the teacher for all of the kids. . . . And that's how they all got involved? Is that right?"

He invited her out to Reform and the base to see for herself.

"Could I get a ride in an F-15E too?" she asked.

"I'll check with Public Affairs," said Colonel Whaley.

211

"No fair," said Trey when he found out. "I got her to come here. I should get the ride."

The local TV report opened with a shot of Young Oaks.

"Inside these lackluster buildings and rundown exterior . . ." began the report, with a close-up of the rust on the Young Oaks bear, ". . . lies a story that gets to the heart of things. . . ."

The day after the TV piece aired on the local news, the School Commission announced that they too would be visiting Young Oaks. Mrs. Heard greeted them at the door and showed them every inch of the school.

The *Reform Chronicle* wrote up both visits:

School Commission, Local News Organization View Thousands of LGM (and up to 5,000 Cracks) at Oldest School in the District

Each member of the Commission bought several LGM. They agreed, though, that the cracks needed further study — perhaps two or three studies. They called the news station and offered to do a follow-up interview about their proposed solutions.

But the local news did not call them back. Its video had been picked up by a national news organization, which teamed up with them to do a follow-up piece. The national news interviewed Marc in the rehabilitation wing at Walter Reed Medical Center. He showed them how his artificial foot attached to his leg and the exercises he was doing to get stronger. He talked about the other airmen and soldiers there with him. At the end of the interview, he held up a little green army man and mentioned Miss Loupe and some members of Room 208 by name.

The national news team then talked to people who had sent donations and letters, from Maine and Louisiana and Wyoming and California. From Ohio and Florida and Rhode Island and New Mexico. They filmed Mrs. Heard in front of the U.S. map she was repainting, state by state, outlining each one as Room 208 received a donation from someone who lived there. Utah, Kansas, Connecticut, Tennessee.

"Go VOLS!" said Bo when Mrs. Heard outlined the state in bright orange.

At rehearsal, Bo taught Gari how to salute, first the right way, and then the wrong way.

"Right way! Wrong way! Right way! Wrong way!" he drilled her.

Gari begged Melissa to rewrite the script.

"No," said Melissa. "You're good. You really are."

And so, by early spring, Room 208 had collected 99,999 "yesses," which meant that 99,999 little green men and women had joined the first LGM, who was still quietly guarding a framed quote on Miss Loupe's desk in Room 208.

When they heard, Gari, Bo, Melissa, and Trey went to Miss Loupe. Melissa showed her the play she had almost finished writing. Trey showed her a sketch of the program he was design- ing. Bo and Gari acted out the opening scene for her, and Gari, with Bo proudly looking on, demonstrated an extraordinarily awful fall.

"Will you direct the show?" they asked.

Miss Loupe put on her soft black slippers and said her loudest YES of the year.

Not long after, Bo's dad finally got official word of his assignment. He would be going to the Combined Air Operations Center in Korea.

"Korea?" said Bo.

"That's a long way from Paris," said his mom.

"Are you kidding?" said Gari.

"It's a remote assignment if I take it for a year by myself," said his dad. "But if we accept for two years, I can bring my family with me."

"When would we go?" said Bo.

"Early summer."

"Before my mom gets back?" said Gari. "So . . ." She was already forming a plan to go to Korea with Bo and Uncle Phil and Aunt Donna, and then fly back when SeaJA started in September and stay with Tandi until her mom finished her deployment. But she didn't say anything. Yet.

"What do you think?" said Bo's dad.

"I think I need more thinking time," said his mom. She turned to Bo. "What about you?"

"Me?" said Bo. "I get a vote?"

His dad cleared his throat.

"You can vote when you're eighteen," he said. "But I would still like to know how you would feel about this family saying yes."

Bo framed his answer carefully. "Could we go to Hog Heaven? I can't think on an empty stomach."

"Yuck," said Gari.

"They have vegetarian banana pudding," said Bo. "And beans."

They all got in the car together.

30
THE UGLY COUCH PLAYERS PRESENT . . .

THE NEW RECRUIT

An Improvisation in Several Parts
Written by
Melissa Paperwhite
and
The Students of Room 208

With many thanks to
Miss Loupe
for helping us row far from the shore

Sponsored by
Hog Heaven
"Go Ahead. Go Whole Hog."

Program design by Trey Obermeyer

The Audience
(gathered in the cafeteria)

Proud parents and assorted siblings, grandparents, and other relatives of the players, including, of course, Colonel and Mrs. Whaley;

most of the sixth grade (except Dillon, who sent a postcard from Germany);

Principal Mary Heard (who was clutching a large box of tissues);

twelve wiggling first graders in their own special seats up front;

Mr. Eric Browne of Los Angeles, California, who had earlier that day looked at both one Ugly, Ugly Couch, and one rundown theater in downtown Reform;

one Expeditionary Medical Group (by video link from Iraq);

one Special Forces Operational Detachment Alpha, at an undisclosed location (who would watch it, many weeks later, on tape);

Young Oaks teachers from every grade, and their spouses and children;

Mrs. Purdy, who had painted her fingernails gold for the occasion;

Gunnery Sergeant Patrick Yancey, U.S. Marine Corps, Retired, grandfather to Allison Yancey and president of the local POW-MIA chapter;

Airmen Peters and Kresge, both in uniform, sitting with Miss Candy;

a reporter from the *Reform Chronicle*, who estimated the crowd at "up to 600 excited students, friends, parents, teachers, and supportive townspeople";

Mr. Nix, who fell asleep during Act Two; and

Miss Loupe, wearing a tangerine shirt, sitting between her parents, and

her brother, Special Forces Sergeant First Class Marc Loupe.

Backstage
(also known as the cafeteria kitchen)

I can't find my script! My script! Yes, I put it *right there* and now it's . . .

How's my hair? Is it okay in the back? How about the side? The front? Okay, how about the back again . . . ?

She's not going to make it.

Do you think anyone will notice that I'm wearing two different shoes? I think Indy ate —

Oh, my gosh . . . I'm losing my voice. . . . I'm losing my voice. . . . I'm losing . . .

Do you see him? Is that him? No, *him*, sitting next to *her*.

Who ordered pizza? Get that out of here until after the show!

Hey, somebody tell the couch to break a leg. Ha ha!

She's not going to make it.

No, you're supposed to be GREEN, not pale lime. Put some more face paint on . . . and don't forget your neck and . . .

Don't leave the trumpet there! Somebody will step on it!

If she doesn't make it . . .

Five minutes, players, five minutes!

I feel sick.

Pre-Show

. . . Small knots of parents waved and greeted one another; programs rustled as they were opened and searched for names; digital cameras purred in standby mode. . . .

"Please sit anywhere you like."

. . . Tennis shoes and combat boots and sensible square-toed pumps and dainty heels and loose flip-flops all crossed the highly polished floor. . . .

"Go ahead, find a seat."

. . . The mayor arrived, speaking urgently into his cell phone.

"This way, sir, we have a seat reserved for you."

Feet and more feet tramped down the hallway; folding chairs unfolded to make an extra set of rows. . . .

The mayor was still talking into his phone: "Bring her to the door! Flash your lights, if you have to!"

"This way, this way. There are a few more seats back here."

The doors to Young Oaks thumped open, and open, and open, again.

"I'm sorry. There are no more seats. Do you mind standing?"

The mayor closed his phone.

A woman in digitized army fatigues stepped from a Reform County police car in the Young Oaks parking lot.

"Thank you for the ride," she told the officer.

She ran into the school between two giant oak trees with fresh yellow ribbons. A student met her in the hallway.

"This way. Gari's backstage. She's got the trumpet."

The Introduction

Melissa consulted her notebook.

"Good evening, ladies and gentlemen, ma'ams and sirs. Welcome to the Ugly Couch Players' production of *The New Recruit*, brought to you by the students of Miss Loupe's Room 208.

"We would like to thank Mrs. Purdy for the use of the Young Oaks cafeteria in which to stage this show. We would also like to thank Miss Candy and Airmen Kresge and Peters for their help in building the set; Sergeant Obermeyer and his maintenance unit, for lending us floodlights from their night work crew while they are deployed; and to everyone who generously gave to our goal of raising one hundred thousand dollars for the care of wounded troops. This night is our thank you to you, and to all who serve."

There was loud applause at this. She looked down at her notebook once more. "Oh! A BIG thank you to Mr. Nix, who sat guard all night, watching over our set."

Then she closed her notebook and spoke directly to the audience.

"Miss Loupe didn't tell me to say this, but she wants to start a youth theater camp here in Reform. And we want to help her. The grant she's applying for says she must have community involvement. That means US. And it means YOU."

She waved to Miss Candy, who was now standing behind a video camera at the back. "So if you want to help, see a member of the Ugly Couch Players after the show. And if you like our play, JOIN IN!

"Thank you, and enjoy the show!"

The Show

Silence. Lovely, expectant, hardly breathing silence. Then:

The sound of one brown shoe and one black shoe walking. A figure came out of the cafeteria kitchen, pushing through the break in the temporary curtain that reached from wall to wall. The figure entered a taped rectangle on the floor. Everything was dark, except for a circle of light around him. Bo lifted the mouthpiece of an oversized paper trumpet to his lips. He blew. Instead of music, there were words:

BO: Birdie, birdie, in the sky!

The first graders rose quickly from their seats, surprising everyone.

First Graders: Dropped some whitewash in my eye!
BO: Ain't no sissy, I won't cry!
First Graders: I'm just glad that cows don't fly!

They threw out their arms and pantomimed swooping and soaring. The audience rumbled with scattered laughter.

The first graders bumped back into their seats. Bo took the paper trumpet from his lips and stared at it.

BO: Wow. I had no idea it could do THAT.

More laughter.

Bo walked out of the Taped Space and over to Miss Loupe.

The spotlight followed him. He handed her the trumpet, and she blew into it.

This time, the sound of Reveille came floating out from backstage. The sound of a real trumpet, played by a real soldier.

Awake! Awake! it called.

More spotlights flooded the temporary stage with light as the curtain drew back. Row upon row of little green men and women stood at the ready, all 100,000 of them, carefully arranged on wooden risers painted stone gray.

Bo reentered the Taped Space and felt the audience come with him, even as he kept his back to the crowd and faced the thousands of LGM arrayed in front of him. He tucked his hands behind his back and squared his shoulders. A deep, booming voice rolled out of him and echoed through the cafeteria. He paced to the far side of the Taped Space. Every few words, he turned and paced in the other direction.

BO: NOW, LISTEN UP, NEW RECRUITS, LISTEN UP!
I know you feel PLOPPED down here
and you have NO IDEA who these people are
and you have NO CLUE what is going on.
But I PROMISE YOU, you are here because you are needed.
You are here because someone placed you here.
You are here because you answered a call.
You are here because —

A lone figure rushed onto the stage. The figure wore black and her face was painted green. A bit of toilet paper stuck to

224

her shoe. She looked around, bewildered. Bo stopped pacing and turned on her.

BO: YOU are LATE!

Gari froze, then jumped to a painfully awkward pose of attention.

BO: WHERE HAVE YOU BEEN?

She opened her mouth, but only gasping noises like a dying fish came out of it.

BO: Do you even know WHERE YOU ARE?

Gari hung her head and looked down at her feet. She suddenly noticed the toilet paper stuck to her shoe and tried to stretch one arm down toward it while still standing stiffly at attention. She couldn't do it, and she fell over, a slow collapse of arms and legs. She saluted, with the wrong hand, from the floor.

The first graders broke into hysterical giggles, and the rest of the audience sent waves of warm laughter toward the stage.

Gari's heart jumped up and down. She had to force herself to lie still on the floor as the script demanded. The audience was out there! Everyone was watching! She should feel sick! But to her surprise, she didn't want to throw up anymore. She felt the script spreading out in front of her like a beautiful plan. She saw that her mom had made it out the back door of the kitchen and circled around to slip into her seat.

Bo was beside her, saying his lines easily, loudly, with just the right touch of swagger and boldness. He sounded as if he were making it all up on the spot, but they had been saying their lines, over and over together, for the last several weeks.

BO: You ARE the New Recruit, aren't you?

The audience laughed as Gari, still on the floor, switched her salute from her left hand to her right hand and nodded up and down, up and down.

BO: Ever done IMPROV, soldier?

Gari shook her head no, as vigorously as she had been nodding yes a moment before.

BO: I'm going to need help with this one.

He yelled toward the door at the back of the stage.

BO: REINFORCEMENTS! I NEED REINFORCEMENTS RIGHT NOW!

A chorus of actors jogged out in an orderly line from backstage. They formed up around Gari and pulled her to her feet.

CHORUS: REA-DY! (They saluted.)

BO: Okay. Let's show this New Recruit what to do. First, we need a place —

Gari tugged at Bo's sleeve. She pointed to the audience. Bo turned, as if noticing them for the first time. He lifted his hand above his eyes and scanned the crowd.

BO: Hey, who are all *these* New Recruits?

Bo and Gari faced the audience, followed by the rest of the class. Time to move off the script and into the real improv. The videotape at the back of the room was rolling. Would the audience get it? Would they help carry the show?

BO: Give us a place!
GARI: Any place!

There was a brief, scary moment of silence.
Then someone in the audience called out:
"Main Street!"
Someone else said: "Hog Heaven!"
"The playground!"
"Hollywood!"
"Reform!" said the mayor.
"I will, if you will," said someone from the back.
The audience laughed, and Bo was glad for the split second

to think. What place should he pick? The first place yelled out? The loudest? Did it matter where you were?

Soon, he'd be gone from Young Oaks. Soon, he'd have a new house key attached to his red tag. He didn't know what friends he would have in the next place. Whether or not the Flying Farmer came to air shows there. Or if the pickles were good. He'd find out after they'd flown over the Pacific Ocean and landed in Korea, all of them together, in a place he'd never been before. But for now, he knew where he was.

Awake! Awake! Reveille had called. The audience was leaning forward in its seats. The improv had started, and he, Bogart Whaley, was inside the Taped Space. Everyone he knew was with him.

"Okay, we'll start with Reform," he said. "Now, we need an event. . . ."

The audience started yelling: "Graduation!" "Yard sale!" "A parade!"

Gari looked out at her mom. Her leave was only for a few days, and then she'd have to go back. She had no idea what events might happen after that. Or what battles might be fought. Or what courage would be required.

But for now, they were in a space filled with 100,000 acts of kindness. No matter what happened, she knew exactly what her plan would be.

All the time, Mom. All the time.

31
NEW RECRUITS

On the first day of school, Miss Loupe approached the left edge of the front row of her second-ever sixth-grade classroom with a roll of masking tape. As she crawled on the floor, she began calling their names. Some of them she already knew from theater camp a few weeks before.

Then the students studied pages 1–13 of the Student Handbook. They admired the funny drawings throughout the text, showing them How to Ride a Bus Safely (*That kid's trying to bring a cat on the bus!*) and Prohibited Modes of Transportation on School Grounds (*A tank! No tanks on the playground!*).

Later that week, they learned the "Yes, and . . ." game with the help of some prompts left by members of Room 208 the year before. They took the Ugly, Ugly Couch out for a row. They read to their Reading Buddies from Mr. Nix's first-grade classroom. And their Reading Buddies read to them, slowly and proudly, in Miss Candy's new Reading Castle.

* * *

Not long after, Miss Loupe's brother Marc visited them. Mrs. Purdy made corn muffins for him and the entire school. Marc showed them his artificial foot and told the story of his rescue. He let them look, with his sister's loupe, at the lightning bolt patch that he used to wear. He left a box for them to fill with ordinary things to send to Afghanistan. His unit was home, but another had taken its place.

And one day, Room 208 looked at the names on the bottom of the Ugly, Ugly Couch.

"Who are Bo and Gari?" said Max. "There, under those initials, LGM."

"They were in the play last year," said Trina. "Remember? And Trey and Melissa and Allison and Rick and Zac and Kylie and Martina and Aimee and Sanjay and Shaunelle and . . ." She read all the names under the couch.

"I wasn't here last year," said Max. He picked up a tiny paper star that had fallen out of the cushions.

"Oh," said Trina. "Well, our show will be awesome this year too, you know."

Across the country in Tandi's guest bedroom in Seattle, Gari practiced the last lines of her speech in the mirror before bed: *Vote for Gari! Vote for Plan U (You)!* She'd already rehearsed it over the phone with her mom. She turned off the light and crawled under the comforter. Her mom would be home next week, and then she would finally be back in her own bed.

She lay there a minute, and then crept out to the computer in the living room. She sent Bo an e-mail of her entire speech, and ended it with:

You think anybody at SeaJA will vote for the new kid?

Bo wrote back from Korea.

Dunno. Want me to send the Flaming Farmer to buzz the halls for you?

She replied:

Flying Farmer, Bo. Didn't they teach you anything at your last school?

TO THOSE WHO JUST FINISHED:

OO-GAH! OO-GAH!
Don't panic! You know where you are.
Battle stations! Battle stations!
And you know who's with you.
This is not a drill. This is not a drill.
Yeah, New Recruits, we're talking to you.
Everyone you know is fighting a great battle.
Time to step up. Time to step in.
Time to say yes.

AUTHOR'S NOTE

The Air Force base in this story isn't a real one; it's composed of memories from the many places I've lived and my own imagination. I chose North Carolina because it's a setting that I love, with people that I care about, and because the barbecue and the banana pudding are to die for.

The military community is diverse, with more detail and history and lore than I could possibly contain here. Each branch of service is different; each career field and time in service is unique. Make friends with a military family if you would like to learn more. If you are interested in helping wounded warriors, I suggest looking to the Fisher House Foundation, at *http://fisherhouse.org*.

Some of the improv exercises in this book are based upon ones used by The Second City.

ACKNOWLEDGMENTS

Many thanks to my agent, Tina Wexler, who connected me to Arthur A. Levine Books, and believed in *Operation Yes* when it was but a new recruit. To Doris, who read this manuscript at a particularly low point in the battle. To my editor, Cheryl Klein, whom I trust and admire and would have sought out as a friend if she and I had been in Room 208 together. To Linda Lyle, who first taught me how to say yes. To my online community, who encouraged and instructed and inspired me. To Suzie, who showed me how to fall and kept me centered. To my children, Rebecca and Wade, who followed for years, and now lead. To Mike, who has always been sure of my place in the world, long before I was, and who read each draft as both a scholar and a warrior. I love you. To all those who serve, in classrooms and on battlefields, at home and abroad. To everyone I know who says YES each day.

The Nation that makes a great distinction between its scholars and its warriors will have its thinking done by cowards and its fighting done by fools. — Thucydides

ABOUT THE AUTHOR

In her own Plan A, **Sara Lewis Holmes** intended to become an actress, a diplomat, or a physicist. But then she met and married an Air Force pilot, and that launched Plan B: writing . . . and a lot of moving! She has lived in Alabama, New Mexico, Rhode Island, Mississippi, North Carolina, Germany, and Japan, scribbling poems and stories at every stop. Her first novel, *Letters from Rapunzel*, won the Ursula Nordstrom Fiction Contest. Sara now lives with her family in northern Virginia, where she looks forward to whatever Plan C might bring. Please visit her website at www.saralewisholmes.com.

HER WHOLE WORLD IS CHANGING...

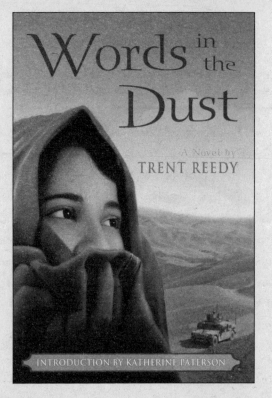

Zulaikha hopes. For peace, now that the Taliban have been driven from Afghanistan. For a good relationship with her stepmother. And to one day even go to school, or to have her cleft palate fixed. When Americans come to her village, they promise new opportunities—and life-changing surgery. Can Zulaikha dare to hope the promises will come true?

"I guarantee it will change preconceived notions about the situation in the Middle East. Highly recommended."

—Teenreads.com

SCHOLASTIC™
Scholastic Inc.

www.scholastic.com

WITD